P9-CLC-835

A Gift from Maine

A
Creative Discovery
and
Activity
Book

This Book Belongs To: _____

Copyright, Trustees of "A Gift from Maine Trust," 1983.

All rights reserved. No part of this work may be reproduced or transmitted in any form or by any means, electronic or mechanical, including photocopying and recording, or by any information storage or retrieval system, without permission in writing from the publisher, except by a reviewer who may quote brief passages for a review.

Published by Gannett Books, Guy Gannett Publishing Co., 390 Congress Street, Portland, Maine 04104, December, 1983.

First edition printed in the United States of America by Gannett Graphics, Augusta, Maine 04330, December, 1983.

Library of Congress Catalog Card #83-083102.

ISBN #0-930096-57-6

A Gift from Maine

by
Maine's Foremost
Artists and Writers
and
James Plummer's
Sixth Grade Class

Guy Gannett Publishing Co.
Portland/Maine

Acknowledgements

A Gift from Maine is the result of the efforts of many individuals. We gratefully thank all the artists and writers who shared their time, talent and enthusiasm with the students who compiled this book.

We also thank the Board of Directors of School Administrative District 15, Principal Gail Gordon, Superintendent Graham Nye and Assistant Superintendent Larry Koch, and the parents of all the children for their encouragement.

Thanks also to the business people and individuals who contributed to the launching of this project; especially to Kinvin and Deborah Wroth for their helpful advice and especially to Joanne Arnold for her design and artwork which wove this book together. And, thanks to Francis Berry for her creative art as well.

The result is truly A Gift from Maine from many people to all who read it now and for years to come.

Dedication

To all the artists and writers who contributed their time, talents and inspiration to the students of the Sixth Grade Class in New Gloucester Memorial School . . . and who thereby made this Gift from Maine possible.

Contributors:

Franklin B. Allen
Joanne Arnold
Dianne Ballon
Edgar Allan Beem
Bill Bonyun
Cissy Buchanan
Margaret Campbell
Mimi Gregoire Carpenter
Marilyn Cartmill
Alfred Chadbourn
Jane Cunningham
Catherine Derevitzky
Martin Dibner
Lew Dietz
Tim Dietz
Jane Dorr
Marilyn Dwelley
Theodore Enslin
Susan Clement Farrar
Sheila Gardner
John Gould
Ada & Frank Graham
Francis Hamabe
Rick Hautala
Robert Indiana
Tina Ingraham
Dahlov Ipcar
Alexander Kemp
Stephen King
James Koller
Patty LaPlant
Kathleen Lignell

Marion Litchfield
Alan Magee
Maine Dept. of Transportation
Maine Fish & Wildlife Dept.
Maine Historic Preservation
     Commission
Maine State Museum
Penny Plumb Mauro
Bruce McMillan
John Muench
Emily Muir
Elizabeth Nieuwland
Bob Niss
Joe Perham
Eileen Rosenbaum
Stuart Ross
Ruth Sargent
Walter Sargent
Nikki Schumann
Lee Sharkey
Marjorie Soule
Phillip Richard Stock
David Walker
Deborah Ward
Linnea P. Wardwell
Neil Welliver
E.B. White
Dorothy Clarke Wilson
Denny Winters
Esther Wood
Jamie Wyeth

Foreword

To read the activities and projects that comprise this work is for me an emotional experience of the highest order. I know firsthand the agony and frustration intrinsic in the creative process. I appreciate the value each artist places on his time and talent. Yet here is a treasure freely given, a priceless gift to the young, an embrace from one artist to another.

Let us hope this act of grace inspires those whom it honors—the artists of tomorrow—to even worthier deeds of accomplishment.

Martin Dibner

A Gift from Maine

Jenny Rickansson
Cheryl Slocum
Deana Webb
Cheri Lavoie
Christine
Marshall
Heather Burrows
Corey Giasson
Brian Hawthorne
James McCarthy
Donald Gagnon
Chris Thompson
Donnie Mooney
Kellie Finn
Rick Kimball
Jon Ray
Heather Kay
Ernestine Drouin
Leah Levasseur
Larry Cole
Ryan Trigg
Lee Jordan
Abe Phinney

Table of Contents

Class time limitations for all the projects contributed by so many generous and talented artists and writers made it impossible to include all contributions in this Volume I of A Gift from Maine.

We gratefully acknowledge the additional contributions sent to us by Margaret Chase Smith, Bill Caldwell, Art Hahn, Joseph E. Brennan, Margaret Dickson, Shirley Lewis, Marlee Carter, Bill Clark, Howard Etler, and Jeanne Titherington among others. We have saved these for Volume II of A Gift from Maine which is being planned and prepared while this first book is being published. Our thanks again to all.

Maine Wildflowers

Contributed by Marilyn Dwelley, Illustrator

Marilyn Dwelley has illustrated three books on Maine wildflowers and trees. She also paints landscapes of Maine places like mountains, rivers, and lighthouses.

When she was a child she drew a lot. When she was in the seventh grade a cousin gave her an oil paint set and she has been painting ever since.

The flowers on this page are some original drawings which were included in her Summer and Fall Wildflower book.

Maine woodlands, fields and roadsides are covered with wildflowers of all colors. It might be fun to draw and find out the names of some of these flowers.

1. On your own pages, make your own book of Maine wildflowers.

Idea: Do your drawings on separate sheets of paper, all the same size. Leave a little bit of a border on each page like this:

When you have completed your drawings you can make a cover like this:

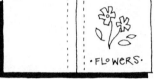

Take a piece of paper *double* the size (width) of one of your inside papers.

Do a drawing on the right-hand side—perhaps you will include a title.

Now, fold this sheet in half on the fold line and put your other drawings (in the order you want) inside this folder. Make sure all the drawings are even inside and right side up.

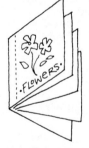

Now close the folder and staple it together like this.

Then get some colored tape—it comes in all sorts of colors: black, red, green, blue, white, etc. Choose a color that will go well with your cover illustration.

Cut a piece of tape about an inch longer than the folded edge of the book. Cover the edge where the staples show with a piece of tape so that it covers both front and back.

With scissors trim the excess tape off top and bottom. Now you've got a handsome book to keep or give as a gift.

Words about Pictures

Contributed by Edgar Allan Beem, Art Critic

As the art critic for the weekly newspaper *Maine Times*, my job is to write about art. There are at least 1,000 artists working in Maine and they each produce different paintings, drawings, prints, photographs, and sculpture as well as craft objects like weavings, pottery, and jewelry, but there are only six or seven people in Maine who write about art in order to help people understand what all these artists are doing.

The art critic's job is to be helpful. To help the public understand and appreciate art. And to help artists produce the best art that they can. The art critic tries to do this not just by trying to tell artists what is *wrong* with their art, but also by pointing out what is good about their art.

The art critic's tools are words...words used to describe, to understand, and to evaluate. Using the picture of the boat made by John Marin in 1932, try writing a critical essay. Here's how:

SAILBOAT
etching, 1932
John Marin

1. Describe this picture in as much detail as possible. For example, what kind of a boat is it? A schooner? A sloop? Is it very realistic or is it just a sketchy impression?

2. To really understand this picture you will have to do some detective work. Who was John Marin? What connection does he have to Maine? What kind of art did he create?

3. What kind of information can you gather about this particular picture? For example, is it a drawing or a print? Pen and ink? Pencil? Lithograph? Is it a typical example of Marin's art?

4. After you have described this picture and have found out as much as you can about it and the artist John Marin, then decide what you think about it. Do you like it? If so, why? If not, why not? Why do you think Marin made this picture? Did he see this boat somewhere? Was he illustrating a story? Did he just make the picture up in his head?

Writing and thinking about art means asking a lot of questions about what we see and trying to find some answers. But remember, just because you may decide you don't like something that doesn't mean it's not good. This is true of many things other than art, but it is particularly true of art. If you are a fan of the Boston Red Sox, you may not like the New York Yankees, but that doesn't mean the Yankees aren't a good team. The art critic's job is to help people understand the difference between liking (taste) and understanding (appreciation). Everyone has different tastes, but everyone should also be able to appreciate things they don't like.

Creating an Advertisement for Yourself

Contributed by Margaret B. Campbell, Illustrator-Designer

Each publication has a certain size specification for advertisements.
Below is a size advertisers use in the <u>Maine Times</u> newspaper. It is 1 column by 4 inch high.

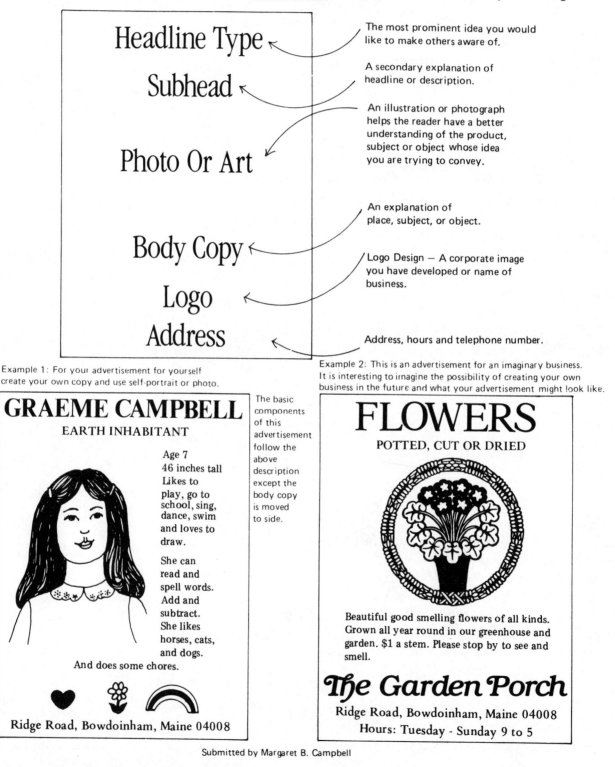

Headline Type ← The most prominent idea you would like to make others aware of.

Subhead ← A secondary explanation of headline or description.

Photo Or Art ← An illustration or photograph helps the reader have a better understanding of the product, subject or object whose idea you are trying to convey.

An explanation of place, subject, or object.

Body Copy ← Logo Design — A corporate image you have developed or name of business.

Logo

Address ← Address, hours and telephone number.

Example 1: For your advertisement for yourself create your own copy and use self-portrait or photo.

GRAEME CAMPBELL
EARTH INHABITANT

Age 7
46 inches tall
Likes to play, go to school, sing, dance, swim and loves to draw.

She can read and spell words. Add and subtract. She likes horses, cats, and dogs.

And does some chores.

Ridge Road, Bowdoinham, Maine 04008

The basic components of this advertisement follow the above description except the body copy is moved to side.

Example 2: This is an advertisement for an imaginary business. It is interesting to imagine the possibility of creating your own business in the future and what your advertisement might look like.

FLOWERS
POTTED, CUT OR DRIED

Beautiful good smelling flowers of all kinds. Grown all year round in our greenhouse and garden. $1 a stem. Please stop by to see and smell.

The Garden Porch

Ridge Road, Bowdoinham, Maine 04008
Hours: Tuesday - Sunday 9 to 5

Submitted by Margaret B. Campbell

CREATING AN ADVERTISEMENT FOR YOURSELF

THIS IS YOUR SPACE.

You can use a separate page to develop a concept for your advertisement about yourself, or imaginary business, or place. Experiment with placing the different components in different places to create the most attention getting advertisement.

Fishmobile

Contributed by Penny Plumb Mauro, Artist

Here's an idea for a "fishmobile" by Penny Plumb Mauro of Deer Isle, Maine. It would be an excellent project for science or marine biology. The commercial fishing industry has always been an important part of the Maine economy.

Materials: Oak tag or cardboard box
Scissors
Paint or markers (color each side)
Fishline or string
Gloss finish if desired

1. Either use the following illustration as a guide or make your own drawings of fish, seaweed, water, etc. on a flat piece of oak tag or cardboard. Cut the shapes out with scissors. Decorate each piece with markers, paint, scraps of colored paper glued on, etc. Loosely hold each piece between thumb and forefinger to find out where they balance (hold them at the top). Carefully pierce a hole at this point of balance with a thick needle or hole puncher. Tie fishline or string through the hole. Balance all pieces from a center piece (such as the water shape on the next page) and attach them to it.

2. Make a fishmobile or design a "Mainemobile" of your own using figures which represent Maine to you. Other ideas could be a Maine Product mobile, tree mobile or people mobile. Design one. They're fun and make great decorations.

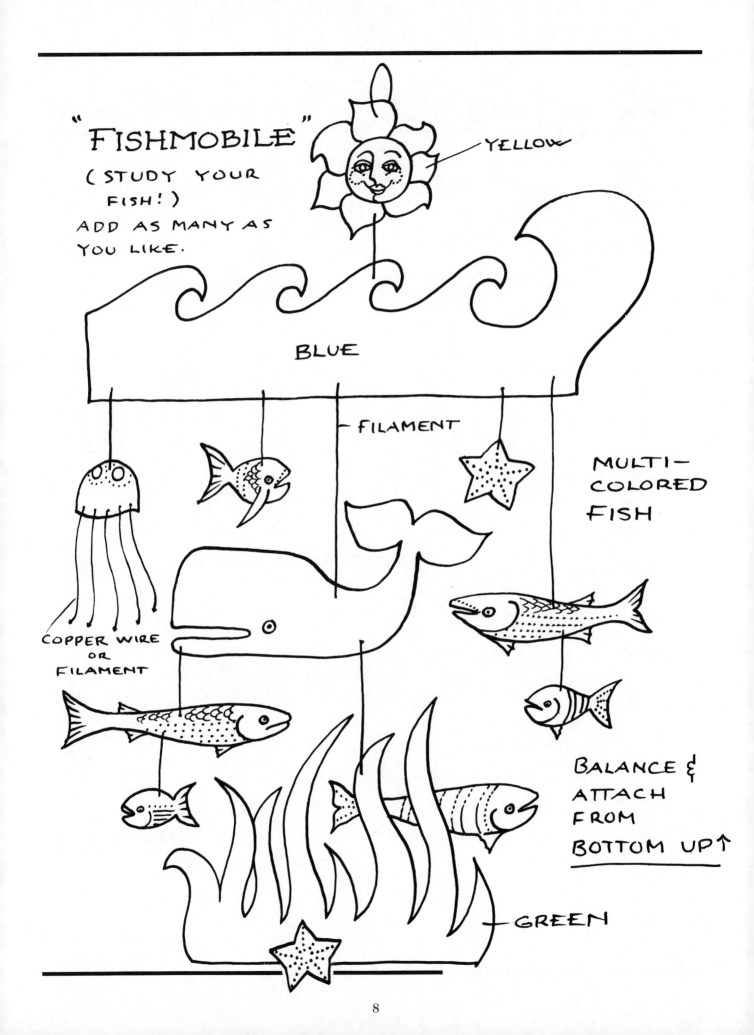

"FISHMOBILE"
(STUDY YOUR FISH!)
ADD AS MANY AS YOU LIKE.

YELLOW

BLUE

— FILAMENT

MULTI-COLORED FISH

COPPER WIRE OR FILAMENT

BALANCE & ATTACH FROM BOTTOM UP↑

— GREEN

Finding Your Way Around Maine

Contributed by Maine Department of Transportation

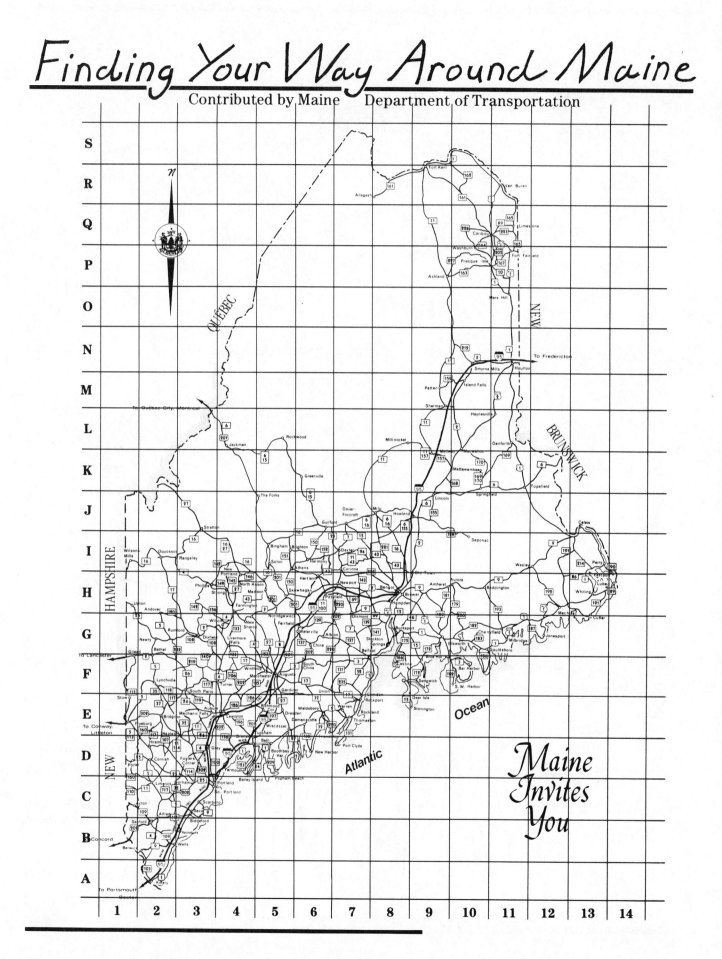

Maine
Invites
You

To find the following towns in Maine use the letter/number guide next to the name of the town. If it says **A2** it means the town can be found on the map in **Row A Column 2.**

Albion	**G6**	Dixfield	**G3**
Alfred	**C2**	Dixmont	**G7**
Allagash	**R8**	Dover Foxcroft	**J7**
Amherst	**H9**	Dresden	**E5**
Andover	**G2**	Eastport	**H13**
Ashland	**P9**	Ellsworth	**G10**
Athens	**I6**	Fairfield	**G5**
Auburn	**E3**	Farmington	**H4**
Augusta	**F5**	Fort Fairfield	**P11**
Aurora	**H10**	Fort Kent	**R9**
Bailey Island	**C4**	Fosters Corner	**D3**
Bangor	**H8**	Friendship	**D6**
Bar Harbor	**F10**	Fryeburg	**E2**
Bath	**D5**	Gardiner	**F5**
Beddington	**H11**	Gilead	**F1**
Belfast	**F8**	Gorham	**C3**
Berwick	**B1**	Gouldsboro	**G11**
Bethel	**F2**	Gray	**D3**
Biddeford	**B3**	Greenville	**K6**
Bingham	**I5**	Guilford	**J6**
Blue Hill	**F9**	Hampden	**H8**
Boothbay Harbor	**D5**	Harmony	**I6**
Brewer	**H8**	Hartland	**H6**
Bridgton	**E2**	Haynesville	**L11**
Brighton	**I6**	Hiram	**D2**
Brunswick	**D4**	Houlton	**N11**
Bucksport	**G8**	Howland	**J8**
Calais	**J13**	Island Falls	**M10**
Camden	**E7**	Jackman	**L4**
Caribou	**Q10**	Jonesport	**G12**
Castine	**F8**	Kennebunk	**B3**
Cherryfield	**G11**	Kittery	**A2**
China	**G6**	Lewiston	**E4**
Corinna	**I7**	Limerick	**C2**
Cornish	**D2**	Limestone	**Q11**
Cutler	**G13**	Lincoln	**J9**
Damariscotta	**E6**	Livermore Falls	**G4**
Danforth	**L11**	Lubec	**H13**
Deer Isle	**E9**	Lynchville	**F2**
Dexter	**I7**	Machias	**G12**

Macwahoc	K10	South Portland	C4
Madison	H5	Southwest Harbor	F10
Manchester	F5	Springfield	K10
Mars Hill	O11	Stockton Springs	G8
Mattawamkeag	K10	Stonington	E9
Mechanic Falls	E3	Stow	E1
Medway	K9	Stratton	J3
Milbridge	G11	Strong	H4
Millinocket	L8	The Forks	J5
Milo	J8	Thomaston	E7
Naples	E3	Topsfield	K12
New Harbor	D6	Topsham	E5
Newport	H7	Turner	F4
New Portland	H4	Union	F7
New Sharon	G4	Upton	H1
Newry	G2	Van Buren	R11
Norridgewock	G5	Waldoboro	E6
North Anson	H5	Warren	E7
Old Town	H9	Washburn	P10
Oquossoc	I2	Waterville	G6
Patten	M9	Wells	B3
Perry	I13	Wesley	I12
Phillips	H3	Whiting	H13
Pittsfield	H6	Wilson Mills	I1
Popham Beach	D5	Wilton	G4
Port Clyde	D7	Winthrop	F5
Portland	C4	Wiscasset	E5
Porter	D1	Yarmouth	D4
Presque Isle	P10		
Rangeley	I3		
Richmond	E5		
Rockland	E7		
Rockport	E7		
Rockwood	L5		
Rumford	G3		
Saco	C3		
Sanford	B2		
Saponac	I10		
Scarboro	C3		
Sedgwick	F9		
Sherman	M9		
Skowhegan	H6		
Smyrna Mills	N10		
Solon	I5		
South China	F6		
South Paris	F3		

Take one box of the graphed map, perhaps the one where your town is located, and make it bigger, about 6″ x 6″ or bigger. Then position the towns inside that box just like they are in the small box. Include places, towns, neighborhoods that aren't listed on the state map. You can illustrate where local mountains, streams, rivers, etc. are located. The bigger you make your square the more details you can add.

Draw your close-up map here or on another sheet.

Symbols

Contributed by Robert Indiana, Painter-Sculptor

Robert Indiana is very well known for his symbol (shown here in a sculpture from his collection):

What do you think he is saying to the world with this sculpture? He uses symbols in his artwork which represent his childhood memories and personal experiences in his life.

He arranges these symbols and numbers in his paintings using lots of thought so that they represent how he feels about a certain subject, like self-portraits of his thoughts.

1. Robert Indiana uses symbols which represent personal feelings. Think about symbols which represent your feelings or goals. Make a list of these symbols.

2. Color plays an important part in attracting attention to his work. For example, red, white and blue may represent patriotic thoughts. The colors yellow and black may signal danger much like a road sign. In his LOVE paintings red, blue, and green attract each other like love itself.

List the colors you would use in a drawing and tell what the colors stand for.

3. Many of Robert Indiana's paintings are in the shape of a circle. The circle is the symbol of his home city, Indianapolis, Indiana. He also feels the circle is a symbol for life everlasting, as is art.

Make a colorful drawing in the circle below using symbols which represent you. The symbols can have very personal meaning to only you.

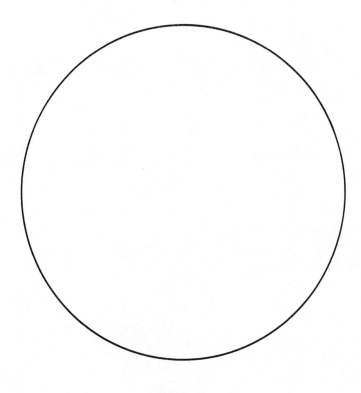

4. What does your drawing mean?

5. Make a poster of your drawing.

Design a Maine Greeting Card

Contributed by Alexander Kemp, Alex-James Greeting Cards

Greeting cards are used every day to communicate our feelings to one another. Often people don't have the time or perhaps the imagination to create messages themselves. There are many different types of cards available today and it is usually possible to find one which says exactly what you want it to say. It can be more fun though, to draw your own greeting card. This makes both the picture and the message even more special for the person who will receive it.

I like to start with an idea for a picture and then think up the words to go inside. It doesn't really matter if you want to do it the other way around. For example, if you are making a birthday card, then you would draw something that reminds you of a birthday. A bunch of balloons or a cake with candles on it would be good choices. You may also wish to include a little person or animal in the picture (perhaps holding the balloons or blowing out the candles) to give it some life.

Some cards in the store just have a picture on the front with no writing inside and this is to allow the person buying the card to write his or her feelings down in that space. When you make your own card, you think up the words by yourself. They could be as simple as "Happy Birthday" or "Merry Christmas", or you could write a short message or verse. If you know the person who you are making the card for quite well, then you can write something you feel about this person and want to share with them. In the same way the drawing could illustrate a particular hobby or interest of theirs in addition to marking an occasion.

YOU'RE SPECIAL!

When I draw I use an ink pen filled with waterproof ink to draw the outlines. This is because I color in my outline drawings with watercolor paint. The ink would wash away when I apply the paint unless it was waterproof. I use a small watercolor brush to fill in the picture with different colors. The paint brightens and softens the image. This is only one method but there are many other ways to draw. You could use pencil and crayons or felt-tip pens or even charcoal. You are only limited by your imagination!

It is always a pleasure to receive a card from a friend but it will be even more appreciated if it is something you designed and created yourself. Make it colorful and think about what you'd like to say inside as you plan your drawing. Don't forget you can always draw cards on a separate piece of paper. You'll find this is a creative and fun way to communicate with those around you!

1. List some people you would like to send cards to.

2. Draw pictures of what you would like on your card. Try to think of a message for the inside.

BON VOYAGE!

3. Now create your card. Make the card special for the person who will receive it.

Suggestion: Sketch your card design here. But you can use any kind of paper folded in half for a card. If you want it to fit into an envelope you already have, be sure to trim the paper you use so that it fits in the envelope before you do your drawing.

 Watching Sea Parrots

Contributed by Ada and Frank Graham, Authors

Parrots in Maine? Some people find it hard to believe, but every spring several thousand small seabirds called puffins arrive on three islands off the Maine coast. There they lay their eggs and raise their young. Fishermen often call these birds "sea parrots" because their huge, fantastic bills remind them of the real parrots that live in tropical forests.

We write books for young readers about nature and conservation. In our spare time we like to watch birds, because in the variety of their shapes and colors and habits they are among the most wonderful creatures on earth. For many years we had heard that a colony of puffins nested on an island not far from our home. We decided to combine our interests in birds and books and write a book about puffins.

Writers are always looking for a fresh way in which to tell a story. Why not tell this story through the experience of two sixth-grade boys who were friends of ours? They were twins, named Roy and Wilbur Hutchins, who had already learned about seabirds by going out with their father on his lobster boat. So, in early June, Roy and Wilbur went with us to live for a week with the lighthouse keeper on a lonely island in the Bay of Fundy where puffins come to nest.

Every morning we went to a little wooden shelter called a "bird blind" that the lighthouse keeper had built on the island's rocky shore. We could look through holes in the canvas that covered the windows and watch the puffins that nested under the rocks. The birds never noticed we were there.

Roy and Wilbur brought their notebooks with them. They described how a puffin flies out to sea and returns with five or six tiny fish drooping from its bill like the tips of a silvery moustache. They drew pictures of a puffin's bill—shaped like a big, three-cornered false nose that a clown might stick on his face to make people laugh. Soon the boys began to realize that this huge, powerful bill, with its sharp notches, enabled a puffin to catch large numbers of fish and bring them back to feed its chick.

Roy and Wilbur kept a record of the week they lived with puffins. They helped us to write our book *Puffin Island.*

A puffin's strange bill is a tool with which it catches fish underwater. Each kind of bird has a bill that is shaped to help it gather food. A woodcock pushes its long, thin bill into the soft ground to find worms. A sparrow crushes seeds with its short, stubby bill.

1. Can you draw six birds that have differently shaped bills? Does each kind of bill give you a clue as to how that bird "earns its living?"

Painting Beach Rocks

Contributed by Cissy Buchanan, Painter

I have always loved the ocean and the beach and the beach rocks. I always returned from a day at the beach with my pockets filled with irresistible treasures, rocks of every color and shape imaginable. I would put the most interesting ones on shelves or window sills to be enjoyed by my family.

One day while looking over my collection, it occurred to me that one of the rocks looked just like a sleepy, curled up cat. I couldn't resist getting out my paints and trying to turn that smooth gray stone into a furry, green-eyed cat. To my surprise, it turned out quite well. Since that day I've painted hundreds of rocks, all sizes and shapes, from very tiny to some so large and heavy I could hardly lift them.

Painting beach rocks is not difficult and it can be fun. For me, the first step is the most challenging and the most fun. Go to the beach or any place where there is a good assortment of rocks. Look at them very carefully. At first you will probably only see rocks but keep looking. Take a few small odd-shaped stones and turn them at different angles, stand back and squint at them. It's really exciting when you finally spy a cat or lion or an elephant. Those are some of the easy ones to find. Among the unusual rocks I've painted are a buffalo, a school bus, and an Indian moccasin. You might like to start with something very simple like a lady bug, strawberry, cucumber or owl. As you progress, you may want to try a basket of flowers, a blue bird, or an Indian in feathered headdress. In choosing a rock, some things you should consider are the smoothness and whether it has a level bottom and will stand up, or if it will lie flat like a paperweight.

After you have selected your treasure, take it home and give it a bath in some nice warm soapy water. Be sure all the soap is rinsed off and let it dry thoroughly. Probably your rock will have some imperfections or will be rough or perhaps need a little help to stand up. Modeling paste will correct these problems. You may rub a bit into the rough areas or apply a couple of coats with a soft brush. Dip the brush in water and run it gently over the paste to smooth it out. When it is completely dry, sand the rock to a silky finish.

Now you are ready to paint. Acrylic paint seems best. It dries quickly to a tough finish and cleans up with soap and water. You don't have to be an accomplished artist to turn out a painted rock. Your painting technique may be very detailed and realistic or quite simple or even stylized like a design. It may help to find a picture of the subject you have chosen.

After the paint is dry, you might like to apply a protective coat of varnish. While most of the high gloss varnishes are very difficult to manage, the companies that make acrylic paints also put out an acrylic varnish in gloss or matte finish. It is simple to use and provides a good protective finish.

The last step is to glue a piece of felt fabric to the bottom of your rock.

That's all there is to it! Oh, incidentally, don't forget to sign your name on your masterpiece.

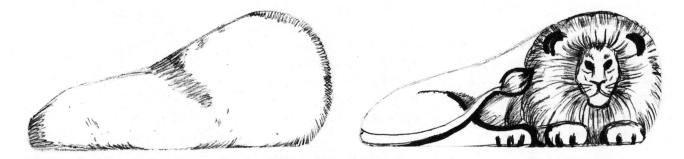

Making A Calendar

Contributed by Nikki Schumann, Poster Artist

I began making posters when I was very young for my friends and family and for school activities. When I couldn't find a reason to make a poster, I would letter a poem or a quotation and draw a picture around it. The felt marker pen was invented when I was in the sixth grade and I was thrilled. In college, I learned to silk-screen and after that I could print hundreds of posters at a time. When I decided to try to earn my living making posters, I had the idea of printing a calendar. I have now made a set of these calendar posters every year for eight years. At first I silkscreened them, but now I make original paintings which a printer photographs and reproduces for me.

To come up with ideas for each month, year after year, requires some stretching of my imagination and powers of observation. I make lists all during the year of ideas as they come to me and then during each season, I sketch and photograph my ideas from the real subject. I usually paint three or four final versions before I am entirely happy with one. As an example of this process, I might think that strawberries would make a good summer theme, and I might imagine what strawberries look like, but when summer comes and I can finally hold a real one in my hand, I can appreciate its full beauty and try to paint it. Though I paint in a fairly realistic way, I don't think this is important in developing good subjects and ideas for a calendar project.

When you work on this project in your own style, look at the ideas you have for a certain month, objects, feelings, weather, things you like to do, and then choose your favorite idea. Think about what makes that idea special for you before you draw it. Use a blank page for a rough draft of your ideas and thoughts, using words and sketches. Then when the month comes it will be time to make your poster with pencils, paints, crayons or markers.

You will need to fill in the days of the week and the numbers under each day. Look at a current calendar to find out which day of the week the month starts. When you have found this out, write a "1" under the correct day and fill out the rest of the numbers like the one on the opposite page.

August

sun	mon	tues	wed	thurs	fri	sat
			1	2	3	4
5	6	7	8	9	10	11
12	13	14	15	16	17	18
19	20	21	22	23	24	25
26	27	28	29	30	31	

Perhaps if you are especially happy with some of your calendar pages, you can make them into larger posters.

Keeping a Journal

Contributed by Esther Wood, Writer

In her book *Salt Water Seasons*, Esther Wood writes about her childhood in a small coastal Maine community six decades ago. She tells about family and village life the way it used to be in the early twentieth century.

She also writes about many things that have not changed since her childhood days—the seasons, warm friendship, family ties, and a sense of belonging.

Esther Wood wrote her book from a journal she started keeping when she was ten years old. She thinks all children should keep some kind of a journal and here are some of her suggestions.

A journal isn't like a diary. It's not filled with "Got up in the morning. Brushed my teeth. Ate breakfast." and things like that. Try to write things that affect you in some way. Include things that you don't want to forget.

YOU DON'T HAVE
1. To start it at the beginning of the year.
2. To write in it every day.

YOU SHOULD SAVE A SPACE
1. To list books you have read, clubs to which you belong, concerts and lectures you have attended, family events, and birthdays of friends.
2. In which to copy quotations that amuse you or inspire you.
3. To paste in a favorite poem or cartoon.

YOU SHOULD
1. Use your journal to record more than events.
2. Use it to relieve your feelings of regret, or sorrow.
3. Use it as a practice book in which to write short stories, essays and poems.
4. Use it as a record book. Record in it your grades, the date you wrote a letter to a relative or friend, the date you started your garden or went on an outing or started a project.
5. Use it as a sketch book. Now and then illustrate an entry with a drawing.
6. Include digests of books and talks which have influenced you.

7. Now and then use your journal as a reminder-book. At the beginning of a new year or month or week, write down what you hope to accomplish in the period. Later check off what you do.

A journal is something that you should enjoy writing in, or adding different things to . . . so you should put things in it that particularly interest you, not necessarily what you think should be in a journal.

Use this page by beginning to write entries or by pasting in favorite cartoons, letters, notes, etc.

A journal is usually kept in a separate notebook or sketchbook. So get an empty school notebook or a blank page sketching notebook (found at bookstores and art supply stores). This keeps all your entries together and allows you to "look back" at old entries from time to time. You might even see yourself growing and changing.

Creating a Picture Story Book

Contributed by Dahlov Ipcar, Writer-Illustrator

I am really more of an artist than a writer, and almost all my picture-story books have begun with some basic idea of some subject I would like to make pictures of, something I would enjoy painting and exploring in more than one painting or illustration. I've made books about lots of different things: farm animals, underwater life, bugs, birds, and merry-go-rounds just to mention a few. After I pick a subject, I try to write a story to go with it.

When I did *Lobsterman*, I thought of all the colorful things I liked about the Maine coast. The fishing villages close to the shore, the different boats in the harbors, the bright-colored buoys, and the piles of traps. Even the gear the fishermen wear is colorful; bright yellow slickers, black hip boots. I also thought about the sea gulls flying all over in clouds and the other shore birds; the seals and the porpoises that you see from boats as you cruise among the islands; and under the water all the wonderful marine life; lobsters and fish, rocks with snails and sea urchins and long streamers of kelp.

1. Perhaps an activity might start that way: think of something you would like to make pictures of, and then write a story to go with it, or a poem.

Exploring the Coast Of Maine

Contributed by Catherine Derevitzky, Illustrator-Author

For several years my husband and I lived on a large 1912 river boat. It had all the conveniences of a home, was 80 ft. long, 20 ft. wide and had been converted to diesel power. We lived on it year round with a dog, Jason, and a one-eyed cat, Scrounge. We cruised the coast of New England from Long Island Sound to Penobscot Bay, anchoring off many islands and going ashore to explore. Much of our food we caught in the ocean or collected on the beach. The *Lobster Pots and Sea Rocket Sandwiches* book was the result of these years. We kept several field books on board the boat to identify new plants and creatures and learn what could be done with them. I would always sketch any new finding.

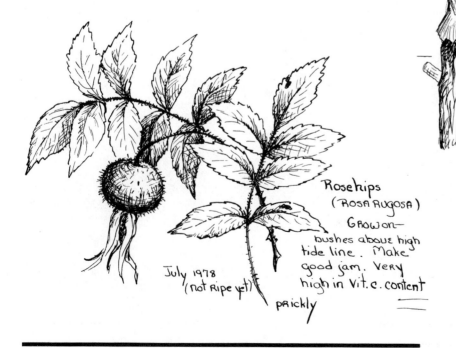

Cormorant
Common bird, seen flying low above water. Perch on pilings. E. Boothbay
June 1977

Rosehips
(ROSA RUGOSA)
GROW on—
bushes above high tide line. Make good jam. Very high in Vit. c. content

July 1978
(not Ripe yet)
pRickly

1. Maybe you have explored some place of your own and found an interesting discovery. Draw a picture of the place you explored and tell of the discoveries you have found.

June 1977

Sea Spinach
(Atriplex patula)
Good boiled as spinach.
Found just above high tide line.
mealy leaves

How to Stencil a Maine T-Shirt

Contributed by Francis Hamabe

Stenciling was done as long as 4,000 years ago. It has been done on furniture, walls, clothes and even important papers such as birth and wedding certificates. Here in New Gloucester there are a number of homes that have stenciled walls that were done about 200 years ago.

This activity has been written so you can learn a little about stenciling, by stenciling a T-Shirt. You will need the following supplies:

T-Shirt
Piece of wax stencil paper or mylar
X-acto knife
Piece of window glass
Fabric paint
Piece of sponge
Masking tape
Sheet of fine sandpaper

First draw or trace your design onto the wax stencil paper or mylar. (If your design has two colors you will need two stencils, one for each color). Now using your X-acto knife, cut out the design, using the glass as a cutting surface. After you have your stencils cut, place the sandpaper inside your T-shirt rough side up; next tape stencil onto outside of T-shirt over the sandpaper.

Now you should place a small amount of paint onto the glass. Using the sponge, pick up a *small* amount of paint and gently dab over stencil until area is lightly but evenly covered. Carefully remove stencil and place second stencil into place and repeat process with second color. Now remove stencil and let dry. After T-shirt is dry, remove sandpaper and iron to make paint colorfast.

Note: *Please* be careful whenever you use X-acto knives and window glass!

1. Work on some ideas for a stencil. Often, stencils use *simple* shapes for flowers, leaves or geometric shapes. But how about coming up with a blueberry stencil, or a lobster or fish stencil? Draw something you like to look at for a stencil. You can even combine several simple drawings for a more complicated stencil. Just remember to keep the drawings *simple*.

Take a Nature Walk

Contributed by Catherine Derevitzky, Illustrator-Author

The study of Nature is the study of the natural world around us, perhaps even ourselves, since we are a part of nature.

Many of the things you find in nature around you, you can bring home. An enjoyable activity would be to go for a walk, and anything you find interesting, bring home and identify in a field book. Many field guides do not tell you of edible and medicinal qualities of a plant so you should look further in more specific books.

It is good to make sketches of things that interest you most. You learn more about them, and have something to remember them by in the future.

Make notes of time of year, where found (swamp, empty lot) and your impressions (smell, texture, etc.)

Design a page using things you found when you took a
nature walk.

Draw a Maine Storm

Contributed by Emily Muir, Artist-Writer

Emily Muir designs houses, paints pictures, writes books, and does mosaics. When she gets in the "doldrums" she likes to draw and paint pictures of wind and storms and angry seas with zigzag lines and lightning. Her drawings and paintings express her feeling of Maine and nature.

Below is a sketch by Mrs. Muir showing a storm on the Maine coast.

1. Draw your own picture of a Maine storm. It could be a bad snow or rain storm. You could be waiting for the school bus or just looking out your window at home or you could have been camping. Include people and how they struggle against the powerful storm. Make sure you include your feeling in your picture.

If the storm feels sharp try drawing it with sharp lines, angles and marks. If the wind is strong how does it affect a field, trees, water, animals etc.?

Maine Animal Tracks

Contributed by Maine Fish and Wildlife Department

1. CANADA LYNX	8. GRAY SQUIRREL	15. BEAVER	22. OTTER
2. BOBCAT	9. RED SQUIRREL	16. COTTONTAIL RABBIT	23. MUSKRAT
3. HOUSE CAT	10. CHIPMUNK	17. SNOWSHOE RABBIT	24. COW (DOMESTIC)
4. RED FOX	11. WEASEL	18. RACCOON	25. WHITETAIL DEER
5. DOG	12. FISHER	19. SKUNK	26. MOOSE
6. COYOTE	13. MARTEN	20. PORCUPINE	27. PHEASANT
7. BLACK BEAR	14. MINK	21. WOODCHUCK	28. RUFFED GROUSE

Prepared by Klir Beck
Revised 1975 by Cindy House

Perhaps you have seen some of these tracks made by animals in the woods or in the snow. But how would you feel if you came across a track that *no one* could identify?

1. First, imagine and draw a track that you've just seen in the woods. You can use the Maine Animal Tracks as reference but make yours unique and different.

2. Now, draw the animal that made the unidentifiable tracks. Is it big? Small? Hairy? Furry? Vicious? Friendly? What color is it? Etc.

Ballet (boys, don't turn the page!)

Contributed by Susan Clement Farrar, Writer

Upon retirement after forty years of dance involvement, I started to write about what I knew and loved best—ballet.

My first book, *Samantha on Stage* (Dial, N.Y., Scholastic, N.Y., McRae, London) deals with ballet, friendship and understanding people of different cultures. I visited the U.S.S.R. and attended the Bolshoi (Russian Ballet) so the references to customs are authentic.

I was proud to receive the International Book Award and Children's Book Council Award because it told me that young people enjoyed my book. I have also written a sequel called *Bravo, Samantha; Emily and her Cavalier*, and *Clowns in the Kitchen*.

I keep fit by teaching aerobics, choreographing ballets and conducting Stress Labs, my expertise being in the field of movement and relaxation. I also continue with my writing.

My sincere desire is to interest boys in ballet. It is such a misunderstood art form.

Edward Villella, a famous ballet dancer, lived in a very tough neighborhood in Brooklyn. In his youth he was a fine athlete. In college he was a welter-weight boxer.

One day he had to take his sister to her ballet class in Manhattan. He became fascinated with ballet and started attending classes. Of course he kept it a secret from his friends for fear of being labeled a "sissy".

Now that he is a famous dancer he conducts workshops in inner-city schools for boys, demonstrating the big jumps, air spins, and steps of elevation showing boys the speed and skill dancing takes—and exposing them to the joy of dance.

Moves at the Ballet Barre

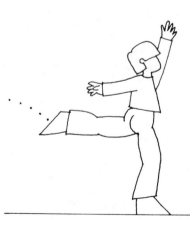

The Language of Ballet is French:

Demi plié (half bend)

Grand plié (big knee bend) stretches achilles tendon so you can leap high in air.

Arabesque sauté (kick with hop) jump up high and land on one foot, kick other leg back.

Grand battement front (big kick) try holding leg straight out front for 10 seconds then lower *slowly, slowly* to floor. Repeat, raising leg to side waist high. Repeat, raising leg to back waist high.

Changement leap straight up in air and land in plié. *Back straight.* Do 50 times like a bouncing ball.

Grand jeté (big leap) run and leap into air, legs extended into a split.

Every step of elevation should begin and end with a plié (knee bend) to prevent injury. A dancer must be very positive. So, instead of saying "I can't do it!", a dancer remains positive and says "I can't do it, *yet!*"

1. The entire class attempts to slowly and deliberately do the ballet steps described. If you can get a dancer to demonstrate, so much the better as there are many important technicalities that are difficult to describe through diagrams.

Great discipline is necessary in ballet—an experience which serves one for a lifetime in all phases of work. Each morning and afternoon a dancer must work out at the barre for 90 minutes and then rehearse dance combinations in the center for several hours. If they are in a dance company they do eight performances a week.

2. Find a book in the library on the Great Ballets which will be described in three acts. Write the story line in your own words describing the situations in a way that colorfully portrays the characters and situations. A misconception that many have about ballet is that it is very somber and serious. *Au Contraire!*

For example: In *Graduation Ball*, the awkward Head Mistress is played by a man. When he dances a *pas de deux*, or dance for two, with the rolypoly Cadet Headmaster it is very comical. In *Cinderella* the Three Ugly Sisters are played by men dressed in silks and marabou. They are ridiculously funny trying to flirt with the Prince!

   a. Either listen to the ballet of your choice on record and envision the ballet as you've described it, or

   b. Illustrate a stage setting in color of the chosen ballet.

3. Arrange for an interview with an Athletic Coach. Find out what the prerequisites are for an athlete. Choose a sport (basketball, tennis, football, etc.) and compare moves in the sport to ballet moves you have done or seen.

Drawing What You Really See

Contributed by Alfred Chadbourn, Painter

This sketch of Kennebunkport, Maine, was done by artist Alfred Chadbourn. Mr. Chadbourn thinks that by drawing sketches you can truly capture the atmosphere of Maine along with your feelings for Maine.

He suggests that before doing a drawing you observe or study what you are going to draw. Notice the important shapes of things you are going to draw. He says, "It's important before you put your hand to paper to first reduce everything in front of you to line, shape and value, (black, white and grays). Squint (your eyes) to see these essentials first, then you will have a clearer idea of what these elements will look like on paper and not what they appear to be in Nature."

KENNEBUNKPORT
MAINE 12 AUG 62

1. Make a simple still life set-up. This can mean a simple arrangement of 3 or 4 objects. Let's say an apple, a banana and a book are arranged on a table.

2. Squint your eyes and notice the simple overall shapes of these objects. Forget about details for now. Notice instead if the shapes are circular, triangular, tall and lean, low or stubby etc.; even notice the shapes created between the objects. This takes a little patience.

3. Now, draw these general shapes as they appear to you on a piece of paper using pencil, charcoal or pastel. Don't add any details until you are quite certain that these general shapes actually look like the general shapes you see when you squint your eyes at the still life. As you draw keep going back to the still life to check your shapes. Don't be afraid to make changes in your drawing to get it closer to what you are seeing. Remember not even really great artists get it right the first time.

The Thing Poem

Contributed by Deborah Ward, Poet-Instructor

We write poetry for many reasons. Ask any poet and he or she will give you a different answer. Some say they can't help it—they write because they are filled with emotions that need to be expressed. The way we express emotion is often by description, and the most useful and brilliant descriptions in poetry are often born of some sort of comparison. When my class at the Breakwater School wrote poems describing emotions I told them to use *things* to illustrate what they meant. One girl wrote: "When I am sad I feel like the only building in the city." She also wrote, "When I am mad I feel like a hot pot of coffee." This is a real *illustration* of emotion because it gives us an object to *see*. Observation is one of the most important gifts a true poet needs to have. We must write from our emotions by the use of our senses. An exercise I find both fun and imaginative is writing the "thing" poem. In this type of a poem we go one step further than the emotions by actually pretending to be the object—get inside it and look out! What do you see? How does it smell? Do you taste anything? Can you hear? Using all your senses in imagining the secret life of that "thing" will give you a new and refreshing way to look at the world. In one fourth-grade class we imagined that we were geodes—a geode is a split stone with crystals and colors inside it. From this exercise we came up with a wonderfully strange poem in which each student contributed a different vision. Here's the poem:

If I were a geode I'd glitter in the blue sun.
I'd eat the letters of the alphabet, drink
the months of the year. I'd smell the blue fresh air.
I'd hear the cave's water dripping.
If I were a geode I'd hear the snakes singing.
I'd see a lot of pink spiders.
I'd smell purple moss growing on the rocks.
If I were a geode I'd smell the orange fires.
If I were a geode I'd live the life I could.

1. Think of an object. Just look around the room—it could be something as simple as a pencil. Imagine you are the pencil, use your senses, think in terms of sounds and colors, shapes and tastes. Don't necessarily tell the truth. Go deeper and deeper into the object where anything can happen and your imagination will create a wild

and beautiful poem. One class in describing a potato called it "A teardrop from a giant having a good cry." Compare your thing to other things. Make it visible, give it moods and other characteristics.

2. Read the poems which are examples of both famous poets and student work. Enter the imaginary life-force of the object and begin to dream!

Stone

Go inside a stone.
That would be my way.
Let somebody else become a dove
Or gnash with a tiger's tooth.
I am happy to be a stone.

From the outside the stone is a riddle:
No one knows how to answer it.
Yet within, it must be cool and quiet
Even though a cow steps on it full weight,
Even though a child throws it in a river;
The stone sinks, slow, unperturbed
To the river bottom
Where the fishes come to knock on it
And listen.

I have seen sparks fly out
When two stones are rubbed,
So perhaps it is not dark inside after all;
Perhaps there is a moon shining
From somewhere, as though behind a hill—
Just enough light to make out
The strange writings, the star-charts
On the inner walls.

Charles Simic

Things

Hard, but you can polish it.
Precious, it has eyes. Can wound.
Would dance upon water. Sinks.
Stays put. Crushed, becomes a road.
(stone)

Mine to give, mine to offer
No resistance. Mine
To receive you, mine to keep
The shape of our nights.
(pillow)

My former friend, my traitor.
My too easily broken.
My still to be escaped from.
(mirror)

To support this roof.
To stand up. To take
Such weight in the knees...
To keep the secret.
To envy no cloud.
(wall)

Donald Justice

The Pillow

The pillow is like a soft
    mountain.
The pillow looks like a
    round ball.
The pillow looks like green
    hair.
The pillow is like a small dot
    floating in the air.
The pillow smells like a fresh
    flower.

Joshua Miller (4th grade)

What is a Logo?

Contributed by Joanne Arnold, Illustrator-Designer

A logo is like a trademark. They help us to recognize certain companies. It is difficult to go through a day without seeing a logo. Look around and you will see logos on your cereal and cookie boxes, on cars and trucks. Even ski resorts and the Maine Mariners use logos. The artwork in a logo gives us clues about what the name means or what a company or person does.

Below are logos of some Maine companies. Have you seen any of these?

A logo to me is much like a poem. In a poem a poet must choose words with a lot of care so that each word counts and is important in getting across the message. In a logo an artist must make every line, shape and color count and be important so that people will pay attention to it and recognize it.

1. Design a logo for a Maine business, it can be a real business or one which you make up.

First, decide on a business _____.

2. What drawings will help explain what the business does?

3. Think about somehow combining the name of the business with a drawing.

Being Famous (or not so Famous) in Maine

Contributed by Neil Welliver, Painter

About this activity Mr. Welliver wrote:

"This is not a joke. My name and picture are often in newspapers and national magazines. I am paid very well for my work. Sometimes I envy people who farm, or cut wood or fish, etc. Can you imagine why?"

These are his suggestions about discovering what makes someone famous:

1. Pick a person you know who *is not* famous.

First, reverse all your questions about being famous.
2. Write some information about this person. What do they do? Who does it influence? Does what they do affect people positively or negatively?

3. Draw a picture of this person doing what they do.

4. Many people who are famous wish they were not. What does it mean to be famous? What price does one pay for being famous? What price does one pay for being rich? (A good joke would be to say, *"Any price you like!"*)

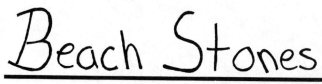

Beach Stones

Contributed by Alan Magee, Painter

When I paint beach stones I am very interested in the individual textures, patterns and colors of each stone. I have found that the best way for me to paint these fascinating stone surfaces is to allow the paint to drop, spatter or flow onto the canvas or paper. These naturally flowing patterns are very similar to the patterns formed in nature by the flow of molten stone, or the stippled look of blue-gray granite.

In painting stones I have two problems to solve. They involve:

Texture—To give a stone visual interest.

Shading—(light to dark) to give a stone volume and weight.

1. Color this drawing of stones using some unusual methods to apply colors to the drawing. Try spattering some of the stones with watercolor onto the drawing using a wrinkled piece of tissue or paper towel or perhaps the palm of your hand. To protect finished and still white areas of the drawing you can make a stencil or window mask for each large stone using a piece of tracing paper or wax paper. Just trace the outline of the stone you want to spatter and cut a window out of the tracing paper. Try to think of some methods of your own for painting various textures.

2. Shade the drawing of stones after they are colored using a very sharp black pencil. Remember when shading that your light source is consistent and all stones are light on the same side and dark on the same side.

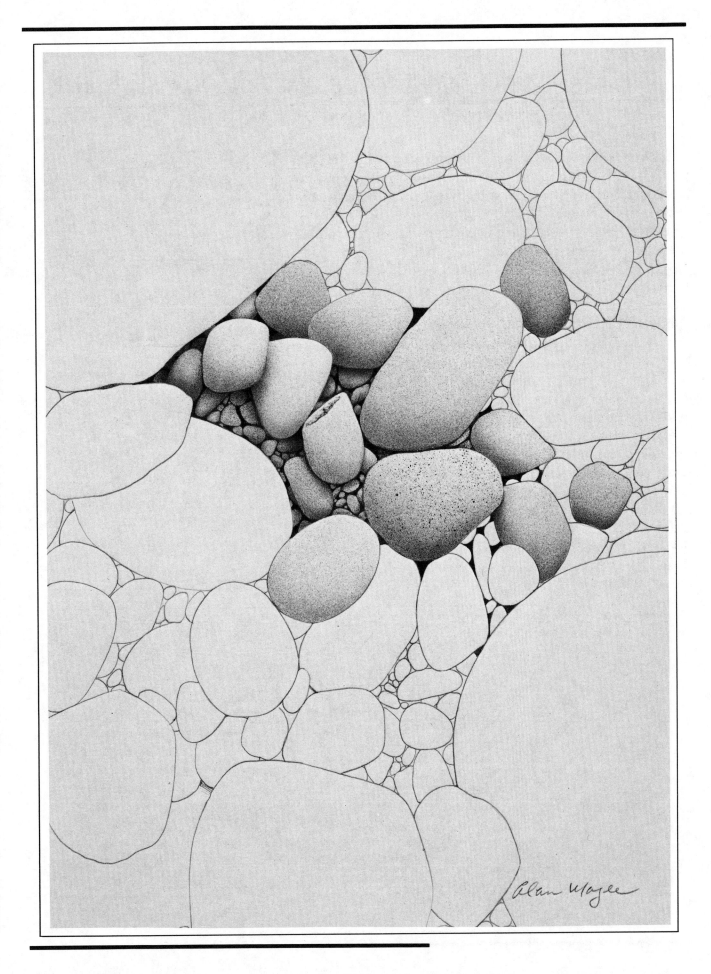

Make a Book About Your Town

Contributed by Mr. Plummer's 6th Grade Class

This Is New Gloucester is an activity book for kids published by sixth graders in James Plummer's class at Memorial School. It includes history, games, diagrams of canoes and houses to cut out and put together and drawings. They wrote their book to make the history of their town more interesting to young children. Each Maine city, town, or village has its own fascinating history that you can put into a book of your own. The place where you live may have been a harbor on a coast where fish were plentiful and ships could easily sail in and out. It may have bordered a great forest whose trees could be felled, dragged out, and milled into lumber for homes. Or perhaps the soil promised productive farming. Some spots enticed settlers with the possibilities of mining gold, silver or copper.

History involves many questions that need to be answered. Sometimes it takes a great deal of detective work to uncover the right answers. For instance: Why was your location settled? How was its name chosen? Does the name honor a certain person, such as Jackson Heights or Watson's Junction? Or was it in memory of the place the people had come from, such as New Gloucester, Plymouth or Yorktown? Does it have an Indian or ethnic name? What does it mean?

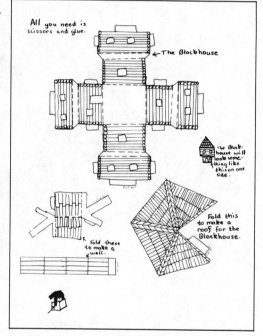

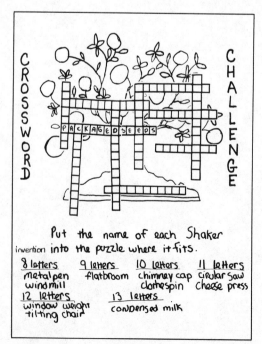

45

The History Of _____

Its name _____

Reason _____

_____

It Was Founded In _____ By _____

_____

Population During Its First Years _____

Interesting Items to Include In Book (*Indians, forts, pirates, people, landmarks, etc.*) _____

_____

_____

_____

_____

Industries _____

Recreation Sites

    Lakes _____ Rivers _____

    Ski Slopes _____ Other _____

_____

People & Groups Who Can Help You Find Information:

Books In The Library:

An Imaginary Maine Animal Story

Contributed by E. B. White, Writer

"I have been asked by Mr. Plummer to tell how the creative process works, but I don't believe I know how it works. When a mosquito bites me, I scratch the bite to relieve the itch, and when I write something I guess I am just trying to get rid of an itchiness inside of me. If you put a young child down on the seashore, he usually tries to create something out of the sand—he builds a castle or a bridge. If you take a dog to the seashore, he doesn't try to create anything, he just wants to destroy the castle or retrieve a frisbee. It's a difference in itchiness.

A good way for a young person to be active is to keep a diary, or journal. When I was young, I began writing about my experiences and keeping a record of my thoughts and desires. Almost every day, I wrote something in the journal. If I was worried about something, I told what I was worrying about. If I was afraid of something, I wrote about my fears. If I went somewhere, I told where I went and whom I met and what I did. I found that I liked writing. It exercised my mind and relieved my feelings. I still have my journal—millions of words. I sometimes read parts of it to bring back memories. I can recommend keeping a diary or journal. It helps you learn to write, and it stirs up your mind in a good way."

Many writers begin to write at a very early age. As they grow older they find they can make a living by writing. Writers often write their thoughts down on paper in words and pictures. Sometimes it takes years before they finish writing their story and have it published.

E. B. White likes animals and enjoys spending time on his Maine farm. When he was feeding the pig one day he began to feel sorry for he knew it was going to die. Mr. White used his imagination and started to think of ways he could save the pig's life. Children everywhere are now delighted when they read *Charlotte's Web*, the story about a girl named Fern, a pig named Wilbur, and Wilbur's friend Charlotte, a gray spider who lives in the barn with Wilbur and saves his life. Although Mr. White's story is imaginary, he likes to think there is truth in it, too.

1. Maine is full of fantastic characters and events which would make good stories. Think for a minute of an animal you would like to write a story about. Draw a picture of this animal and where it lives.

2. Do some research in the library about your animal. List all the facts you can find about the way your animal lives.

  Suggestions: What does the animal eat? Where does it live? Does it hunt? Does it live alone or with a family? Does it have enemies? Is it threatened by man in any way? Are there certain things this animal loves to do?

3. Create a short story about your animal using the facts you found in the library. Try to create an unusual personality for your animal.

When there is Nothing to Write About

Contributed by Eileen Rosenbaum, Writer-Instructor

The activity I would like to suggest is one I use when students tell me, "There is nothing to write about." Each of you has an untold number of ideas and memories in your mind; the trick is to "hook" one as you would a fish. By capturing one of your life experiences, you develop the ability to communicate clearly and with feeling. Most writers of fiction—even those who write fantasy and science fiction—use their own experiences in their writing.

Each of the following "thinkabouts" is meant to remind you of some experience you may have had. Read each one, then pause and think about it. If it reminds you of some experience you have had, write a sentence which will identify the experience for you until you can come back and write about it more fully. If the activity works, you should end up with a list of ideas you can make into pieces of writing. These pieces may stand by themselves, become poems, parts of stories or even plays. Don't forget to include description and dialogue:

1. Think about a time you were alone and very frightened.
2. Think about a time you went on an exciting ride.
3. Think about a time you said something and later regretted it.
4. Think about a place you like to go to be by yourself.
5. Think about the best moment you ever had with a pet.
6. Think about the funniest meal you ever had.
7. Think about the best present you ever *gave*.
8. Think about the best present you ever *got*.

9. Think about the most interesting room you've ever seen.

10. Think about the most dangerous thing you ever did.

11. Think about something you can do better than most other people.

12. Think about something that happened in school that made you proud.

13. Think about a time you helped someone and felt good about it.

14. Think about a time you failed at something you were trying to do.

15. Think about a time you were hoping for something and felt very disappointed.

16. Think about the worst argument you ever had.

17. Think about a person who can do something which interests you.

18. Think about a time when you had to make a difficult choice.

19. Think about something in your room which means a lot to you.

20. Think about something someone told you which you will never forget.

There they are. If you've taken your time with them you should have a number of ideas to write about. And now you may be able to invent your own "thinkabouts" for yourself and your friends.

Sounds in Poetry

Contributed by Theodore Enslin, Poet

Theodore Enslin is a Maine poet who has published over 63 books of poetry. He also writes short stories.

He says that writing poems comes from many sources at once. It depends on what one knows about language, and how to use it, upon where you live, how you see familiar things, on interests the person writing the poem has, and it may involve many other things as well.

Mr. Enslin says that after nearly fifty years of writing, he thinks he knows less about where his ideas come from, or ways to encourage ideas, than he did when he started. He doesn't say this to discourage you in any way. It certainly doesn't discourage him! He thinks that it is very exciting to have no idea of what he may be writing tomorrow. Most of us write poems sometime or another during our lives, or at least want to. He says writing is like planting a seed. After it has been planted, it takes patience to see the mature plant.

So what does he tell us that will help?

1. Make a list of words that come from actual sounds of an object or action...what we call onomatopoeia...the list is endless and some people think that all language started that way. Anyway, listen to words as sounds, just as you listen to tones in music, and the length of the sound will help you come up with more words.
Some examples are:
sizzle (listen to the sound of bacon cooking)
chickadee (the sound of the state bird)
buzz (the sound of a bee)
What do you think of when you hear the following sounds?

hiss _____

quack _____

oink _____

2. Now, listen to sounds that objects or actions make and list some of your own.

3. Write a poem using words as sounds.

A Blueberry Picture

Contributed by Phillip Richard Stock, Painter

People from all over the world enjoy blueberry pie, muffins and many other desserts and breakfast pastries made from blueberries grown in the state of Maine. The state of Maine grows more blueberries than any other state.

1. Draw a picture with blueberries in it.

Ideas: What is your favorite way of eating blueberries? In a pie? Over ice cream? How do blueberries grow? What does a blueberry field look like? Who else eats blueberries besides people? Blueberries are special because of their color. How many other things do you eat that are blue? How do blueberries look when they are lined up in quart boxes at a fruit stand? What does a fruit salad look like with blueberries in it? What is it like to rake blueberries?

Something that made Me Laugh

Contributed by Elizabeth Nieuwland,   Writer

Anyone who wishes to write must be a good listener and a good observer. It helps to read a lot too.

I write about things that actually happen, I just exaggerate quite a lot. For instance, one of my stories was about getting a cat down from a tree. It was late at night in the middle of February, and very cold. I stood on a chair in the middle of the sidewalk and held a broom up on the tree hoping that Albert, the cat, would get on it and I could bring him down. After he finally got down, I wondered what would have happened if a policeman had come riding by and seen me! He would probably wonder why I was hitting the tree!

Also I noticed that I spent all my time letting my three cats out the door and in the door. So I wrote that I had hired a man to come to the house and do nothing but let the cats in and out all day!

So read, listen, observe, and use your imagination.

Write a story about something that made you laugh. You can exaggerate it and use your imagination to add to your story if you would like to. Draw a picture if you wish.

Write a Curiosity Poem

Contributed by Theodore Enslin, / Poet

Theodore Enslin suggests: "Be aware of everything, always...be curious about things, about people, about sounds." He says that the one thing that artists and writers have in common is curiosity. Curiosity about everything. Curiosity is the desire to learn or to know about something. Write down something you are curious about.

1. Start with the words "I am curious about _____ ."

2. Then write a poem of any length about why you are curious.

3. Your rhyming pattern could be AA, BB, CC.
   I am curious about the *ocean*
   Maybe it's because of all the *motion*.
   The water comes and *goes*
   Where to nobody *knows*.
   I wonder what is at the bottom of the *sea*
   The world hidden from you and *me*.
   Think of all the secrets that it *holds*
   Maybe someday they will *unfold*.

Now you write a curiosity poem.

Remembering Your Dreams

Contributed by Theodore Enslin, Poet

Another thing Mr. Enslin has found valuable when he writes is to remember as many dreams as possible. No one really knows why it is when we dream we can see things that are not there, but we can. When we dream we can see things we wish would happen. Sometimes we see things that frighten us and we hope they won't happen. Sometimes the things are so different we can't figure out why we dreamed them.

Close your eyes and relax. Imagine something which you plan to do this weekend. Did you get a picture? Dreams happen in much the same way, but come when we are asleep.

Keep this next page open some night and when you wake up see if you can write down everything you dreamed.

Use this page as a journal to write down your dreams. See if you can write a story or draw a picture about your dreams.

Maine Comparisons

Contributed by James Koller, Poet

James Koller is a Maine poet who has been writing since he was 10. He believes that a poet is like a door or window through which pieces of the world must pass before they become poems. Most of what he writes about he has seen or heard. To write about something, you really have to look at it closely while you have the chance.

When writing, Mr. Koller sometimes compares something to something else. In his poem below he compares a tidal river to a yellow dog drinking. He wants to make you hear the sound of the water, and also feel the friendly nature it shares with most yellow dogs—on this particular day in any case.

Now the poem:

Coming up the river coming in
with the tide coming slow
water slapping at the mud, so
gentle, sounds like a yellow dog
drinking water, slow, the birds
getting up, slow, fish, slipping
quick & easy out & back
into the water
      Gonna sleep on board
gonna listen to the river
rock me to sleep. Fireflies.
O slow & easy, rock me
to sleep to sleep. Fireflies.
July 1978 (J. K.)

Comparisons help Mr. Koller describe what he wants to say.

1. Some other examples of Maine comparisons might be:
An *apple tree* gone wild looks like a *cat* gone wild.
Young oak and *pine trees* growing under taller trees are like *children* standing with adults.
A *walk* in the woods in the fall sounds like *eating* crispy potato chips.
The *summer breeze* was as soft as the *whisper* of a friend.
See if you can draw pictures of some of these comparisons.

2. See if you can finish these comparisons:
The snow fell like...
The ice was as smooth as...
The wind was as cold as...

3. Listen to people talk and try to remember some fresh new comparisons you hear. List them below. This is one way to make a poem. Think of a comparison. Then write a poem telling all you can about the comparison.

Write About an Ancestor

Contributed by David Walker, Writer

Try to imagine something about the life, and the personality, of an ancestor in your family, an ancestor that you never knew but whom parents or grandparents can tell you something about. Try to think of how they would live, what they would do, what would worry or please them, whom they might know (Indians, an early President, etc.), and what their world would be like. Try to write something that might capture a moment in the person's life: their son returns from a war, maybe the American Revolution or the Civil War; or their log cabin has just burned; or the ship they were on just arrived from a long voyage; or they've just heard President Lincoln has freed the slaves. Don't try to say "everything" about your ancestor; try to find a good combination of things that would help the reader to know and understand the person and their world.

One way to get started is to get a photograph such as a daguerreotype of an ancestor. Study it. Or does your family have any old letters or other material about an ancestor? I once found a letter, written in 1851, in which my great-great-grandmother said she was about to marry a man who was "six foot four inches tall in his bare feet!" Sometimes just one or two little things can start you off. Above all: use your imagination!

1. Now—write down some information you found about an ancestor.

Did you learn a name? Occupation? Hometown? Family? Birthplace? Year of birth and death? What else did you discover?

2. Use your imagination and write a poem or short story about your ancestor describing what you picture about him or her.

3. Draw a picture of your ancestor. Try to draw details of the time and place in which he or she lived.

Finally—maybe you should go back and re-imagine your poem. Maybe you have new ideas, better than your first ones. Maybe, for instance, you feel like changing something important about what you first wrote: having the ancestor speak the poem, rather than being spoken about, for example. That can be quite exciting. How would a person born two hundred years ago *talk*? This is called "revision"; it means simply, to see again what you are trying to do.

Share your poem or story with others, when you feel it is ready. Listen to their reactions, consider their suggestions. But, do not feel you *have* to change what you've written because others want you to. Remember: a real poet or writer must have the courage to stick by their work as they see it.

An Inanimate Object Comes To Life

Contributed by Marion Litchfield, Illustrator

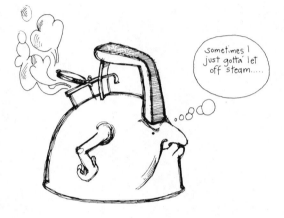

The book *The Littlest Lighthouse* is an imaginary story of how a lighthouse comes to life.

The story takes place on Peaks Island in Casco Bay not far from Portland. Since Portland harbor is the largest and most important commercial harbor in the state, it has many lighthouses large and small and numerous types of boats. When one lives on an island and looks out on the harbor in all types of weather, it is easy to imagine how seasonal and weather conditions might even affect a lighthouse.

When Mrs. Sargent asked me to illustrate her story, *The Littlest Lighthouse*, it was not hard for me. I watched the harbor from our island and closed my eyes, and imagined all the sights and sounds that a small lighthouse might overlook. I made a list of things that a lighthouse might "see", *if it could!* From this list, I sketched various scenes suggested by the story.

It is fun to close one's eyes and picture in your mind what an inanimate (something that is not alive) object might "see" and "hear" under various circumstances. Imagination is a great gift.

For example:

1. A familiar tree (perhaps a very old oak or pine tree).
2. A bridge (your choice might be an old "covered bridge"— or a "draw bridge" over a harbor which opens for many boats).
3. An "antique" (did you ever think of the strange stories an old teapot or a patchwork quilt, or spinning wheel might tell?)
4. Ocean waves (consider the different sights they might "see" of the four seasons—everything from the winter's North Atlantic storms to the calm waters of summer when the happy tourists come to Maine).
5. A ferry boat (on Casco Bay a little ferry boat might "see" many of the sights that *The Littlest Lighthouse* saw!)

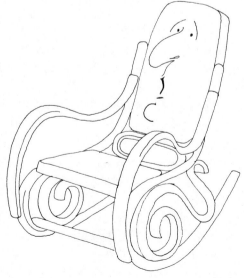

1. Use your imagination and draw a picture of an object you would like to bring to life.

2. List some different things it could "see" and "hear" if it could.

3. Now write a story that your object has to tell.

Maine Events

Contributed by The Maine State Museum

The purpose of this activity is to bring to your attention some of the exciting and romantic events in the history of Maine. Many writers use events of the past to create a story. They do research in libraries and find out all they can about the history of the subject they are writing about.

List Of Historical Maine Events

1605 Samuel de Champlain set up a colony on the coast of Maine, but because of the long, cold winter he left.

1629 The Pilgrims built a trading post in Machias and were able to pay most of what they owed on the Mayflower expedition by trading for furs with the Indians.

1632 A notorious pirate named Dixey Bull attacked a fort at Pemaquid and destroyed it.

1650 Maine was in a great deal of confusion because of Indian raids and pirates attacking settlers on the coast.

1715 Benedict Arnold led an expedition from Augusta to Quebec on foot and the first naval battle of the Revolutionary War took place in Machias when the Colonials captured the English ship the *Margaretta*.

1787 Stagecoaches began carrying people from Portland to Portsmouth.

1791 Portland Head Light was built at Cape Elizabeth. John Greenleaf was the first keeper of the lighthouse and he was appointed by George Washington.

1807 Henry Wadsworth Longfellow was born on February 27th.

1820 Maine became a state.

1838 A terrible earthquake was felt in Maine. It was so strong that it destroyed lighthouses and many chimneys.

1863 Confederate soldiers tried to capture the ship *Caleb Cushing* from Portland Harbor. They were caught by the people from Portland and put in jail.

1866 A fire destroyed most of Portland. Over 1,800 buildings burned. The fire started because of a July 4th celebration.

1888 The first five-masted schooner, named the *Governor Ames*, was built at Waldoboro.

1898 The battleship *Maine* was blown up in Havana, Cuba.

1931 Percival P. Baxter gave Mt. Katahdin State Park to Maine. It is to be preserved in its natural state forever.

1941 Some German spies were captured trying to come ashore on a Maine beach.

1963 President John F. Kennedy visited Maine three weeks before his assassination.

Pick an event in Maine's history that you would like to know more about. Pick one from the historical list or one of your own.

1. Which event did you choose?

2. List all of the facts you can find about this event from the library.

3. Make up a newspaper story of this event as if you were there. Draw a picture and make headlines to go along with your story.

Here's a guide to mock-up a newspaper cover.

The Kid's Times
vol.1, no.1   30 cents   (your town), Maine   (date , 19__)

_____ (headline)
by _____ (your name)
Maine- _____

draw a picture here
or
use a photograph you already have or find one in a magazine

Photo by _____

(put your story here or rearrange the whole page)

(how about including weather or sports news) (make an advertisement) (Contents or another small article)

Weather
Rain today

Sweatshirt Sale!!!
only $5.00
JIM's

the Inside story
Lost Dog Found
.... page 18
School Holidays
.... page 2
Circus in Town
.... page 5

Being a Poet

Contributed by Lee Sharkey, Poet

When Lee Sharkey was in junior high school she knew she wanted to be a poet. She didn't know what being a poet meant exactly, except that she'd write poems and probably be misunderstood. The center of her life is still writing poetry. She owns her own printing press and prints her own books of poetry.

She thinks poetry in Maine is booming. Many writers choose to live here because the state is so beautiful and people leave you alone.

She says that some of her poems come from dreams and suggests that people write about what really interests them and how they feel about things. Also be honest with yourself when putting your thoughts down on paper.

Relax and think about your feelings and interests about some things. Make a list of some of these things.

Now write your own poem about your feelings and interests.

Try to make your feelings as clear as possible to someone who might read the poem. It doesn't have to rhyme if you don't want.

Every Poet is an Ecologist

Contributed by Kathleen Lignell, Poet

Poetry and ecology have a lot in common: *ecology* is the science of the relationships between organisms and their environments, while *poetry* deals with the relationships between the self and one's feelings about his experiences in the world.

Every poet has a different way of expressing in words what he feels about the world. Whether he uses strong *visual images*, or depends on a pronounced sense of *sound*, or breaks up the *lines* of the poems in new ways, the poet is always trying to find new ways to express his experiences by putting words into a form that pleases him.

Ecology is the word we use to talk about saving the animals, plants, and the natural resources of the world for future generations of human beings. The poet is also interested in the future life and welfare of people and their planet. Both ecology and poetry are about concern for the grasses and rivers, the herring in the Bay of the Fundy, the sand dunes on the coast that are slowly eroding into the ocean, and the way that people treat the natural living creatures of the earth.

I write every morning at 4:30 a.m. before I go to my other job as a university editor/writer. Usually, the sun is just beginning to come up when I am sitting down to the typewriter. Every morning I watch the day begin and am reminded of the absolutely balanced system of nature in which we live. At dawn it is very still in the world of nature, and it is also very noisy—there are few cars going by my window and no human voices. It takes a while to realize the amazing hubbub of life that is going on in nature when you are so tuned in to hear man-made sounds all day long.

1. Try to think of some time when you were by the shore or in a forest or on top of a mountain. Write a few lines about what you saw, what you felt, what you heard, what you thought, what you realized about yourself in relationship to the world. Put your lines into groups of lines that seem to hold together, because they are about one thing or one thought. Now you are on the way to writing a poem and understanding how a poet and an ecologist are almost alike.

How to Draw a Lobsterboat

Contributed by Jane Cunningham, Artist

Here's a step-by-step method of drawing a lobster boat.

On this page draw a lobster boat and include some
other colorful things you might see on the Maine coast.

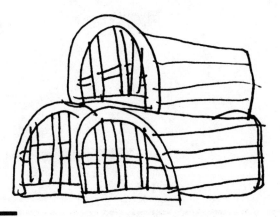

Drawing From Memory

Contributed by Phillip Richard Stock,   Painter

This exercise in drawing from memory will give you a chance to get to know your gift of memory and what it is like. You will see how you can use it to improve your drawing skills the way many artists do. There are three very distinct advantages to being able to draw objects from memory: the first is that you are able to make yourself see what you want, whenever you want to.

Secondly, when drawing from memory you don't have to make the object look exactly like what is in front of you. You can make changes in size and color to please you.

The third and most important thing to remember is that this type of drawing is wonderful for the eye, hand, mind and imagination.

I try to draw an hour a day. I will draw anything and everything, whatever comes to mind. Then I will draw several different versions of whatever it is I'm drawing.

Now to begin. Take an object as simple as a tin cup. Place it in front of you and look at it. I mean really look at it, from the top, all sides, and different angles. Absorb the shape. Now pick it up, feel it, the thickness, the shape, the weight, the size. Get to know it. Get to know what it can be: shorter, taller, heavier, lighter, old, new, full or empty. After you have studied it, put it out of sight.

69

1. Now close your eyes and relax. While your eyes are closed think about the object you were looking at. Let your imagination work.

2. Open your eyes and draw as many versions of the object as you can.

Drawing from memory is a gift many artists use everyday. The more you use this technique the better you will get at it.

Drawing From Nature

Contributed by Linnea P. Wardwell, Illustrator-Artist

My husband, Larry, our baby son, Devan, and I have our home on an island—Swans Island—near Bar Harbor. The island is a beautiful place—still and silent in winter when the bays steam with sea smoke on cold days; and warm and vibrant in summer with lots of wild blueberries and huckleberries to eat. About 350 people live on the island year-round and about 1,000 come to enjoy it in the summer. The ferry takes cars back and forth to the mainland and it runs all winter in almost all weather. You have to time your life around the ferry—it won't wait for anyone!

Swans Island, Me.

I began my drawing career doing sketches for magazine articles and books by the *Mother Earth News*. Then I began sketching and painting the wildflowers and birds living on our island and selling the prints in a small shop we operated several years ago. From that small beginning our print business grew and now we sell thousands of them to shops all around the country. Each of my prints is an original pen-and-ink design which is then carefully printed on the highest quality paper and hand painted in water color. My husband frames them in 5 x 7 natural wood frames and handles all the marketing.

I usually do my drawings on plain white paper and make sure I have a good pencil and eraser. I go out for a walk on the island and find a wildflower or something else of interest. If it's a winter day I might sketch an evergreen branch or dried flower head poking out above the snow. If the plant is large like a rosebush or fruit tree, I might just draw a few branches close up so I get in all the details.

Now, go out and draw from nature yourself. After you have finished a pencil sketch, sit down and ink in all the outlines over the pencil. A fine tipped permanent marker works well. Then gently erase your pencil lines and color in the leaves and flowers with watercolor or colored pencil. Sign your name and you have an original botanical print you can give to someone for a gift.

twinflower
Linnaea borealis

It's fun to draw from nature. Here are two samples of my work which you can color.

black-capped chickadee

L. P. Wardwell

L.P. Wardwell

lowbush blueberry

Vaccinium angustifolium

This page is for you to create nature drawings.

The best thing about drawing from nature is that you look more closely at things you've always seen before and you will appreciate them even more. Hope you enjoy your nature drawing as much as I do.

Impossible Things

Contributed by John   Gould, Writer

"There's no use trying," she (Alice) said, "one *can't* believe impossible things."

"I daresay you haven't had much practice," said the Queen.

"When I was your age, I always did it for half-an-hour a day. Why, sometimes I've believed as many as six impossible things before breakfast!"

Do you believe that this wooden arrow passes through the hole of this board, or is that impossible?

Would you believe that the arrow can be removed from the hole without damaging the arrow or the board? It would seem as though it would be possible since it must have been put through the hole in the first place!

If it is impossible to remove the arrow, how did it get in?

Perhaps it is not important to solve this small puzzle for the sake of an answer—maybe it is more important to keep an open mind about impossibles, and to believe in them!

Pliny the Elder observed: How many things are looked upon as impossible until they have happened.

Suppose you could take a voyage backward in time. Where would you go? Would the people you spoke to believe some of the inventions which we now have? What would they say?

1. When thinking of impossible things you have to use your gift of imagination and think about things in new ways. Can you think of something which is impossible now but you believe might be possible in the future?

2. Think of something which you did that you thought was impossible.

3. It may seem impossible that anything you could do could be important to the whole world. But you have done it. You have accomplished something important.

4. Draw a picture of what you did which many people thought was impossible.

Draw a Special Day

Contributed by Cissy Buchanan, Painter

Cissy Buchanan has always loved Maine, especially the coast. About eight years ago she started painting rocks from the shore and selling them at flea markets and gift shops. This was her first venture into professional art.

Cissy Buchanan says she won't try to tell anyone how to paint since she taught herself, but she will share some of her methods with you. Her style of painting is called primitive. First, think of a happy day, a special day, perhaps a holiday.

1. Think of all the activities that happen on that day. Make a list. What season is it? Think about the colors of that season. Think about trees and flowers and don't forget birds and animals. Try to think of every detail because they count in the whole painting.

2. Deciding how to bring all these things together is like solving a puzzle. You will probably want to try different arrangements on scrap paper. Remember, relax, be yourself. Find your own style and have fun, she does.

Rubbings

Contributed by Stuart Ross, Painter

If you put a piece of paper down on your desk and blacken it all over with a soft pencil, an exact "image" of the desk top will appear on the paper: wood texture, scratches, someone's carved initials, etc. This is called making a "rubbing" and you have probably all tried it. This technique can be used for recording any interesting textured or carved surface. Old gravestones in a cemetery are especially good for making rubbings. They are almost always beautiful examples of the carver's art, and they provide a historical record of their time. The following tips may be helpful.

1. Use light but strong paper. The thinner the paper the clearer the image will be, but it must be strong enough to withstand the rubbing. Experiment with tracing paper, typing paper, rice paper, etc.

2. Tape the paper to the surface you are rubbing, at the four corners if possible. If the paper moves while you are working you will spoil the rubbing.

3. Use a soft, dark drawing material. Art supply stores sell graphite in stick form, pastel chalk, and even a special material made for rubbings. Start at one edge of the paper and make even, gradual strokes, back and forth, moving toward the other edge, so you cover the paper with a good dark tone. The carved lettering and decoration will appear white. Black is the best color for a rubbing, but you can try other colors.

There are other interesting subjects for rubbings, among them: cast iron manhole covers in the street or schoolyard, (*do not* try this on a busy street, and always have a friend watch for traffic), bronze plaques in schools or other public buildings and at the base of statues, decorative titles on buildings, tree bark, auto tires, etc. Use your imagination. Any textured surface will make an interesting rubbing.

Collect your rubbings in a portfolio, and label each one for place and date collected. Get permission to make a rubbing if you think it is necessary, as in a cemetery, and be careful to keep the graphite or chalk on the paper.

Happy Rubbing!

Create Your own Logo

Contributed by Joanne Arnold, Illustrator-Designer

When I create my own logo, I want one that will in some way describe me. Since I know myself best, I'm the expert needed to figure out exactly what types of things will identify me. I love to draw so my personal logo uses very simple drawings of pencils (drawn in a "different" way).

joanne arnold   illustrator

You can even represent yourself by the things that you really don't like. How about this one for someone who hates vegetables?

Or, use the shape of your initials to somehow describe yourself.

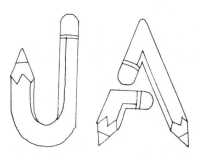

Or, just use the shape of the letters in your initials in a special design for yourself.

Now create your own logo, a personal one that will in some way describe yourself.

1. Make a list of things that represent you or things you like to do.

2. Create a logo for yourself.

3. Design a logo of something you don't like.

Color can play a powerful part in making logos. An artist gives a great deal of thought to which colors will be used in a logo, because they will affect what we feel and think when we look at them.

Be creative with your materials! Use the tools (pencils, pens, crayons, etc.) you enjoy but thinking of new tools to use can help you create different kinds of drawings to use in your logos.

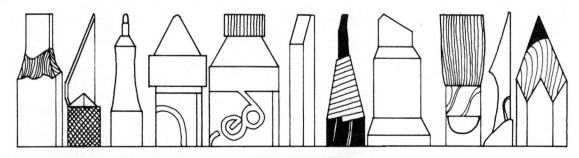

Draw Your Favorite Maine Place

Contributed by Marjorie Soule, Artist

The sketch on the opposite page is the first full view you see of Sugarloaf Mountain as you travel north on Route 27. After playing "hide and seek" among neighboring mountains, suddenly as you round the bend—there it is, in all its glory. That is why this particular spot got to be known as "Omigosh Bend". This is a special Maine place to Marjorie Soule.

1. Try to picture in your mind your own special place and draw it. It doesn't have to be a famous place, just one you remember as special.

2. Write a few sentences telling why this is your favorite place.

Portland Headlight

Contributed by Jane Dorr, Artist

Portland Head Light
Cape Elizabeth, Maine

by Jane Dorr

This sketch of Portland Head Light served as a basis for a large painting by Jane Dorr.

1. Use your imagination and add something to her sketch.

Ideas: What's the weather like? Is it stormy, sunny or somehow otherwise? Are there any animals or people there?

Paint a Maine Pine Tree

Contributed by Tina Ingraham, Artist

You will need: 1. 1″ wide, flat watercolor brush
2. Plant mister or sprayer or empty Windex spray bottle

1. Hold the brush straight up and use the tip for the boughs of the tree. Sweep the brush up and outward for the upper branches of the tree (the lighter ones). On the lower, heavier branches sweep the brush out and downward. Try twisting your brush for the branches that come straight at you. While the paint is still wet, drop in darker colors to define shadows.

2. To give the pine a softer, leafier look, borrow Mom's plant "mister". After your tree is complete, but still slightly wet, mist just the edges of the leaf sections of the tree. Hold your hand over the area not to be misted. Only one or two squirts are needed. Too much will give you a paint puddle! Notice the soft edges on the tree on the right. It's been misted!

3. Draw or paint a picture with a pine tree in it.

Suggestion: Use a piece of watercolor paper which will absorb excess water to paint on, and then glue your drawing here.

Suggestion: Maybe you can do a painting of a close-up of just one branch of a pine tree instead of the whole tree. Notice how the branch is constructed and how the pine needles grow.

Draw a White Tailed Deer

Contributed by Patty LaPlant, Artist

Long before the white men came to Maine, the deer supplied the Indians with meat and clothing. Deer are still found in every section of the state. We don't very often see them in the woods because they are fast and camouflage themselves well. The deer below is a male or buck. The female is called a doe and the baby a fawn.

Using squares to break down a picture is a good approach for a beginning artist. Notice the use of lines, dots, and squiggles to shade the deer.

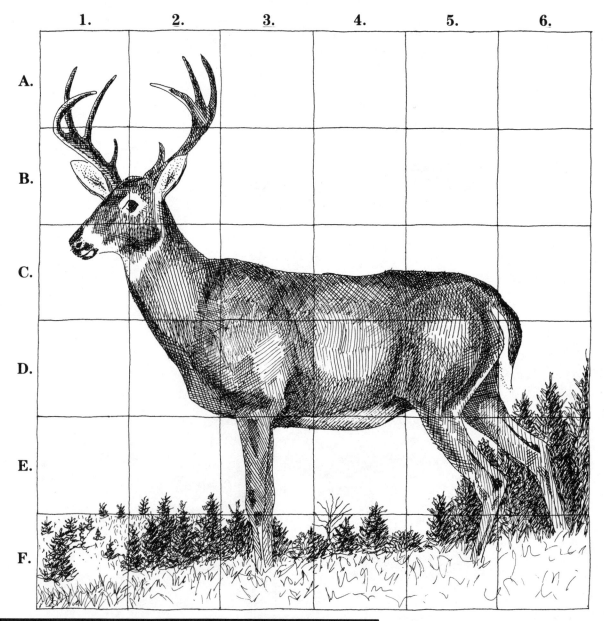

1. Can you recreate the white-tailed deer using these squares to guide your drawing? Draw the outline of the deer lightly at first so you can erase if necessary. Notice that the numbers and letters can help you find out what is in a specific square. Example: Draw what is in Box 1A first, then 1B, etc.

2. Once you have completed the outline of the deer, shade your picture.

3. Find out more about the deer from an encyclopedia. What do they eat? What laws protect them? When are the fawn born? Write a poem about deer.

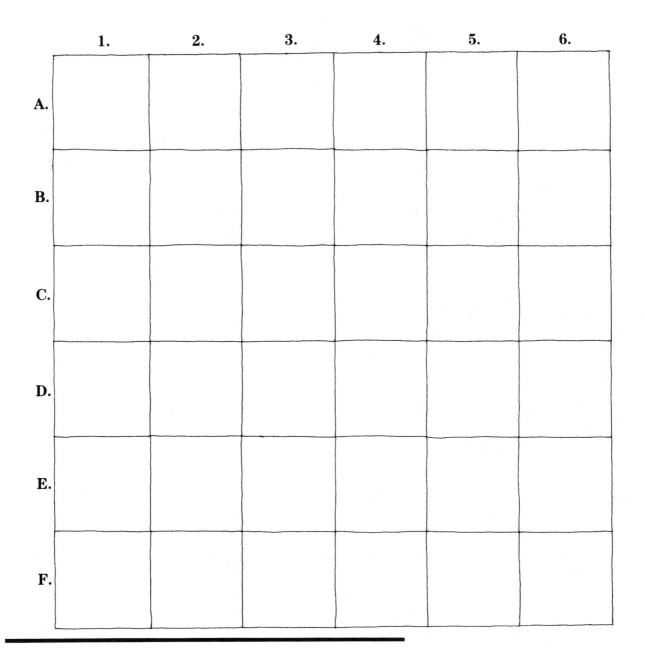

Finding Something Special

Contributed by Mimi Gregoire Carpenter, Writer- Illustrator

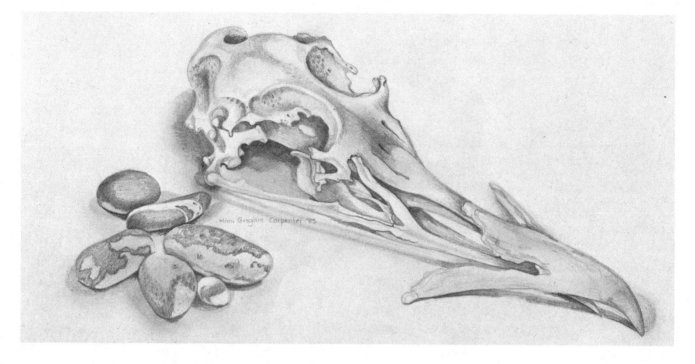

I am an only child and so is my daughter Tessa. We've spent many hours alone using our imaginations to entertain ourselves—as we played, as we drew or as we wrote. Both the books that I have written and illustrated, *What the Sea Left Behind* and *Mermaid In A Tidal Pool* have to do with learning about yourself and your surroundings, about being sensitive and about being creative. If you are not alone, you have to be certain to find some special alone time to discover yourself. My activities are designed to do just that.

The drawing I've included is of some of my favorite objects I have found.

Take a walk alone, on the beach or in the woods, and search for treasures that have a value and meaning which are special to you. Try to take the time to notice and appreciate everything. Hopefully this will help you to understand that whenever you look closely at anything—including yourself—you're certain to find something special.

1. Study the color, shape, and texture of an object you have found and carefully draw it below. Take your time.

Maine Whales

Contributed by Tim Dietz, Writer

These exercises will help familiarize you with some of the earth's grandest creatures—the great whales. With the help of my wife Kathy, these exercises were designed to familiarize you not only with different species of whales but also with their different sizes and shapes. I hope by following these exercises, you'll begin to realize that the great whales come in all shapes and sizes representing the largest creatures ever to exist on this earth.

The whales on this page and the next have been seen in the Gulf of Maine.

COLOR THE WHALES

Finback Whale, 70 feet long, color brown or dark gray

Right Whale, 50 feet long, color brown leaving marked areas white

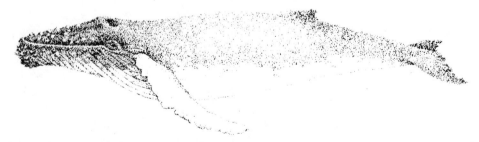

Humpback Whale, 45-50 feet long, color dark gray leaving marked areas white

Minke Whale, 30 feet long, color dark gray leaving marked areas white

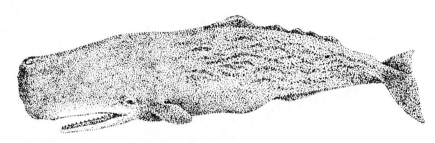

Sperm Whale, 60 feet long, color dark brownish gray leaving around mouth white

The purpose of this exercise is to help you become familiar with some of the most common types of whales.

Match the name of the whale with the correct description by drawing a line.

The following are *baleen* whales (whales with no teeth). Baleen is a filter-type substance which hangs from the roof of the mouth.

A. **Finback**

1. "Large-winged whale of New England". Most acrobatic of the great whales.

B. **Minke**

2. Largest animal ever to exist on earth. Its coloring is pale blue to gray with light irregular mottling.

C. **Humpback**

3. One of the smallest of the baleen whales, ranging from 15 to 30 feet. Scientific name: *Balaenoptera acutorostrata.*

D. **Right**

4. Can reach lengths of 75-80 feet and 50-60 tons. One of the fastest of the great whales. Also called razorback.

E. **Blue**

5. One of the rarest whales. A very slow whale which was easy for whalers to catch. It has no dorsal fin.

The following are *toothed* whales:

A. **Harbor Porpoise**

1. Adults of these species are all white. They have rounded heads, no beak, and no dorsal fin. Normally lives in polar seas.

B. **Pilot Whale**

2. "Flipper" was this type of whale.

C. **White-sided Dolphin**

3. Most commonly seen small whale in the Gulf of Maine, reaching a length of only 4-6 feet. Also called "herring hog".

D. **Killer Whale**

4. Type of whale in "Moby Dick". About 50-60 feet in length. The back portion of the body has a shriveled appearance.

E. **Bottlenose Dolphin**

5. Grows to 9 feet in length. Most distinctive marking is the yellowish streak which runs in an elongated oval from beneath the dorsal fin towards the tail.

F. **Beluga**

6. Has extremely tall dorsal fin up to 6 feet in height. Black with white underside. Also called orcas. The most famous whale of this type is "Shamu" at Sea World.

G. **Sperm Whale**

7. It has a bulbous, melon-shaped head which looks like a large upside-down kettle. Also called "pothead" for this reason.

The following books will help:
Dietz, T. *Tales of Whales*, Guy Gannett Publishing Company, 1982.
Katona, S.; D. Richardson and R. Hazard. *A Field Guide to the Whales and Seals of the Gulf of Maine*, 2nd edition. College of the Atlantic, Bar Harbor, Maine, 04609. Maine Coast Printers.
Also, check any encyclopedias in the library.

Photography: a Childhood Hobby

Contributed by Bruce McMillan, Photographer-Writer

Photography, a childhood hobby, has turned out to be my adult job. I got my first camera when I was in the fourth grade and have been taking pictures ever since. I use photographs in my books instead of drawings. Each can do things that the other can't.

My first book is called *Finest Kind O' Day* and it is about lobstering in Maine. I photographed it while I was a caretaker on a Maine island.

In *The Alphabet Symphony* I shared with children my way of looking at things a bit differently using something they all know, the alphabet, to make a book. In *The Remarkable Riderless Runaway Tricycle* I used photography to tell an improbable story, a story which couldn't happen in real life. In *Apples, How They Grow* I compressed time, a year's growing season, into 48 pages. I moved inside after that to show how something all children wear, "grows" in *Making Sneakers*. In *Ghost Doll*, once again I've used photography to tell an improbable story, a fantasy about a lonely ghost doll and the brave little girl who turns it back into a real doll. A story about an animal journey is told in *Here A Chick, There A Chick*.

I had to make a chicken house after my last book and I now get fresh eggs every morning. *Apples* got me so interested in that fruit I now have 50 apple trees.

I can't imagine going on one of my school visits and not bringing along my tricycle and my ghost doll. I'll leave the chickens at home.

Write a story about one of your photographs.

paste
your
photo
here

Stephen King

Contributed by Stephen King, Novelist

Stephen King is a Maine author who was born in Portland in 1947. When Stephen was eleven, his family moved to Durham. He attended school in Durham and then Lisbon Falls High School, graduating in 1966. He graduated from the University of Maine at Orono in 1970, with a B.S. in English and certified to teach.

He married Tabitha Spruce in January, 1971. He met his wife in the stacks of the library at the University of Maine. Stephen was unable to find a job teaching immediately after leaving college, so he worked in a laundry and wrote short stories.

In 1973, the Kings moved to a rented cottage on Sebago Lake. It was here that he wrote *Salem's Lot* and waited for the publication of *Carrie*.

The Kings have three children.

Mr. King has written several novels and short stories and many of his novels have been made into movies. He has an excellent imagination and writes about things which are sometimes scary.

This Is What Scares Me Most!
Walking through the woods at night
Something watching me just out of sight.
I wonder what could it be?
Something makes me run by the next tree.
Chills start going up my spine
Then I make it home and I'm fine.
Chris Bradbury
Age 11

Write a poem of what scares you most.

"Who likes to Get Scared?"

Contributed by Rick Hautala, Author

Everyone likes to get scared—at least a little, right? Of course I'm right!

If you've ever had to walk home from a friend's house alone...at night, or told ghost stories around a campfire, or—probably worst of all!—walked through a cemetery *on Halloween night*, then you *must* have felt at least a little tingle up the back of your neck, right? Oh yeah, you *know* I'm right!

And I'll go so far as to bet you a week's lunch money that you even thought it was *fun*. Maybe not while you were doing it, but after—once you were safe at home, you let out a small sigh of relief and then laughed.

Then, maybe a week or so later, you told your friends what you saw on your way home—or what you heard in the cemetery. And I'll just bet that you added a little something to your story because you wanted your friends to feel *just as scared as you did.*

...the shadows under the trees, just a little too far away from the streetlight, *really* seemed to move, right?

...the shimmering white shape above the tombstone *really* did look like a person, didn't it?

Am I right?

And I'll bet you thought it was just great when goosebumps ran up your friends' arms and one of them whispered, "Really?"

And you nodded your head and said, "Really!" because there's nothing in the world more fun than giving someone a really *good* scare!

1. Why do you think ghosts haunt the places they do? What are they doing, hanging around spooky, dark, old houses, anyway? Write a little story and tell me, if you were a ghost, where would you haunt and who would you like to scare?

Antiques in Maine

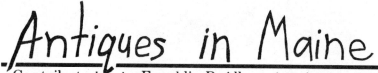

Contributed by Franklin B. Allen, Auctioneer-Appraiser F. O. Bailey Antiques

Anywhere you look in the Maine countryside, you can see that people have lived around here for hundreds of years. You will see stone walls in the woods among the trees, built, of course, before the trees grew; the remains of an old dam on a brook or a river; bankings where old trolley or railroad lines ran through the countryside; old horse-drawn farm machinery in barns, or even out in the fields. Of course, if you happen to live in an old house, there are many parts of the house that had special uses when it was built. The things in your house, even if it is not an old one, may have been handed down from grandparents and before, and be antiques. Some things have obvious uses, but it is hard to tell what some other things could have been used for.

1. There are old containers, tin boxes, bottles, and so forth which have the name of the product and the company on them. Some things will have the name of the maker, and even the patent date of it. If it is a well-known name, such as some of the sewing machine companies, you might be able to look them up in the encyclopedia and find out the dates and the extent of the operation. If it is a local company, such as a bottling plant, you might find it listed in your town historical society.

2. It is interesting to list some of the old things around you. Find out what older family members know about them, and do research after that in local libraries, museums, and books on antiques.

3. There may be an antique dealer in your neighborhood who could answer questions about the pieces for you. It's more fun if you try to look up those things which you like personally and discover their history as well as the way they were used.

Historic Places in Maine

Contributed by Frank A. Beard, Maine Historic Preservation Committee

One of the most important things that the Maine Historic Preservation Commission does is find out where the important historic places are in Maine and have them listed in the National Register of Historic Places in Washington.

What is an historic place?

Usually people think that an historic place is where a big battle happened or where a famous person lived or is a famous old ship like the "Constitution". These are all historic places but there are many other kinds, some probably in the town where you live.

What is an historic place? It is any place or thing that has something to tell us about our past—about the history of our country, our state, our town, our own families or perhaps about the way people lived and worked in the old days. It is important to save these places and things so that we can learn about our past and in doing that learn why we are the way we are.

Can *you* find an historic place?

1. Look around the town where you live for something that might have something to say about the past. Is there an old mill—maybe no longer being used? Draw a picture of it and then try to find out about it. Ask some older people in town about what the mill was used for. What did they make there? How did they make it?

2. Maybe if you live along the coast you will find an old boat or ship lying along the shore. Does anybody remember who built it, what its name is, or what it was used for?

Sometimes an old house is important because it was designed by a famous architect or is in a style that is no longer in use.

Look around you! There are more historic places and things than you think and it's important to find out about them so that others can learn more about their past.

A Letter to Someone Dear

Contributed by Martin Dibner, Novelist

Martin Dibner is a prominent novelist and an authority on Maine art.

Below is his response to our letter.

Can you think of a unique design for a special message or story?

Folklore and Legends

Contributed by Joe Perham, Storyteller

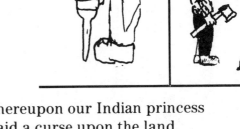
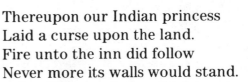

Folklore is stories and folk ways passed down from generation to generation by word of mouth. Folklore is created by groups of people like lumberjacks, Indians, sailors and farmers who use their own special traditions, beliefs and dialects.

A *legend* is an area tale that is told *as if it were true*. A legend often concerns famous people, strange occurrences and haunted houses.

Joe Perham of West Paris, Maine, is a storyteller who performs rural American stories, poems, songs and anecdotes for people of all ages. He incorporates skills as a dramatic actor and stand-up comic with costuming and guitar. A veteran English teacher, he conducts teacher workshops and school residencies in story telling and Maine folklore.

THE LEGEND OF MOLLYOCKET

(to be sung)

At Trap Corner in West Paris
(on the Mollyocket Trail),
You will find this old Maine legend
Truly does prevail.

In the valley Androscoggin
(Little river to the west),
Lived a Peqwakett Indian princess
Seldom known to stop and rest.

Always traveling, ever wandering
(Straight of back and always bold),
Tribal funds she carried with her;
Mollyocket carried gold.

'Til the night came, tired and hungry,
Cold and lonely, Molly knew
That she must bury all her treasure
And find food and shelter, too.

Hanging beartraps o'er the treasure,
To an inn she made her way;
But the owners turned her from them;
At the inn she could not stay.

Thereupon our Indian princess
Laid a curse upon the land.
Fire unto the inn did follow
Never more its walls would stand.

To the Hamlin Home she wandered
There to find both food and rest;
Cured a baby of its sickness,
Then both home and child she blessed.

And the baby, Hannibal Hamlin,
Grew in years, became a man,
Friend of President Abraham Lincoln
And Vice-President of our land.

So (according to the legend),
Molly's treasure ne'r was found;
But, beneath the stately pine trees
Still lies buried in the ground.

(repeat first stanza)

The *humorous anecdote's* purpose is to create a specific effect on the listener—a chuckle or a laugh.

One day my uncle was going from the farm to the village during the mud season (the mud was so deep he had to wear snowshoes). He was about a quarter of a mile out of town when he happened to see in the middle of the road (pronounced "rud") this hat, which as he drew nearer, he observed to be moving right up the road ahead of him. He went over and picked up that hat—and there was his neighbor, Doc Wheeler.

"Doc", he says (pronounced "sez"), "you're in trouble ain't ye?" Doc looks up and says "Nope, I still got my hoss under me."

The point of the *tall tale* is exaggeration.

The smartest fish I ever see was one that jumped out of the water into my boat up to Kennebago. He was only a little fella, so I threw him back, but he jumped into my boat again. Seemed to like riding in the boat, so I kep' him, put him in my bait pail.

When I got him back to camp, I showed him to Russ Crosby. I told Russ that that was *the smartest fish in the world.* To prove it I showed him the fish's high forehead, the wide space between the eyes, and the long eyebrows.

I put him in a big barrel of water and then I started to teach him. I taught him to come when I whistled, and when he come, I'd scratch his dinky little head. Then I'd take him out of the water and let him walk on the grass (at first for only a little while, and then for quite a spell). Finally he was so used to being out of water, he didn't need it any more. That's right! He only used water to drink.

Eventually Tommy (that was his name, Tommy) went with me every where I'd go. By now I'd taught him to speak, to roll over, and to shake fins. Then one day we went down town to git the mail. The path we took ran over this brook. I didn't think nothing of it when I went over that bridge, but there was one plank off...And poor Tommy tumbled through the hole into the water and drowned. I was sad for a long time after that, I'll tell you.

1. Maybe you could write a story about your favorite tale about hunting, fishing, tall tales, tales of the lumberjack and the like or

2. You could write about Maine folklore based on stories you have heard or make original adaptations: smartest fish, dumbest dog, driest summer, coldest winter, and the like, or

3. You could write about the people and events behind the names of buildings, streets, towns, lakes, areas, and the like.

Feel free to draw pictures to go along with your stories!

A Picture Map of Maine

Contributed by | Marilyn Cartmill, Artist

This is a picture map of the state of Maine drawn by the Maine artist Marilyn Cartmill. Picture maps are very helpful if people want to see what is going on in the state.

See if you can find something that begins with each letter of the alphabet in the map below.

A
B
C
D
E
F
G
H
I
J
K
L
M
N
O
P
Q
R
S
T
U
V
W
X
Y
Z

Make your own picture map of the state of Maine. You might want to just include scenic sites, historic places, products, or places you have visited. Or you might want to try to include something from each letter of the alphabet. Try not to overcrowd your map so that it becomes confusing.

A
B
C
D
E
F
G
H
I
J
K
L
M
N
O
P
Q
R
S
T
U
V
W
X
Y
Z

Let's Write a True Life Story

Contributed by Dorothy Clarke Wilson, Biographer

I am a biographer. That is, I write books telling the life stories of real people. After traveling to India, England, and other far places for material, I thought, why not find a subject near at hand? How about that old doctor up in Greenville who has done such interesting things? I wrote to Dr. Fred Pritham, and he agreed to let me write about him.

First I read everything I could find about lumbering and the Moosehead Lake region. I got big maps of the 5,000-mile area where he had been doctoring for over 65 years, traveling by horse, by boat, by car, by train, by wagon, by snowmobile, even by airplane in late years, and thousands of miles on foot. Then I went up to Greenville and spent a month interviewing him with my tape recorder, talking with people who knew him well, visiting many of the wilderness places where he had treated patients, taking pictures.

He has had an interesting life, all right! There were hundreds of exciting stories about his adventures, performing operations in lumber camps with no tools except what he could carry in a basket strapped to his shoulders, jumping trains to get places in a hurry, riding "jiggers", building a snowmobile out of an old Ford car, going through the ice when taking patients to the hospital and nearly drowning them and himself, joining the high school band after he was 65 and tooting his horn in all the school parades.

I gathered all the information, maps, tapes, pictures, came home, and wrote the book, calling it *The Big-Little World of Doc Pritham*, for I wanted to make it not only his story but a history of the whole area and a time which is passing and will soon be forgotten.

I am sure you can think of some person in your town, perhaps a relative, who has done interesting things. Why not go and see that person, ask questions, get him or her to tell you details of life, incidents that would make a good story, and write them down. That is what a biographer calls "research". Of course you need not write a book, as I did about Doc, but if you write just a little about some real person on this page, you also will be a biographer.

The History of the Future

Contributed by Mr. Plummer's 6th Grade Class

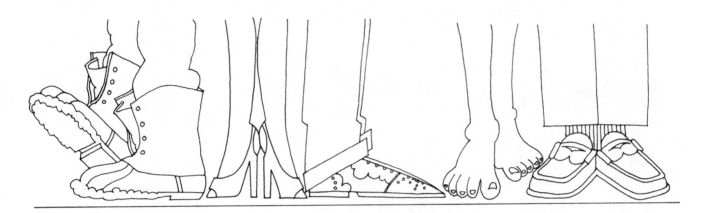

What would you like to do for the history of the future? You may be the mayor someday, or a school teacher. You could be the owner of a service station or a store. You could open a dance studio. You could be a doctor, lawyer or nurse. Every location needs such people. Perhaps you will be one of them.

Do you see yourself as a fisherman? In the military? As a scientist studying lobsters in Maine? Or, maybe it will help to think of the things you absolutely *don't* want to be.

Draw a picture of what you would like to be:

My Creative Process

Contributed by Denny Winters, Artist

Any creative process means expressing something you feel or know in a way that makes others experience it too in some way. Some are harder to understand than others.

When I was around twelve, I was certain that I would be an artist all my life and was fortunate that there was an artist in the neighborhood who let me go out sketching with her and watch her paint in her studio. I learned a lot about being a professional artist. I liked painting nature rather than people and I liked painting autumn best because of the bright colors. Later I learned that I could use color any way I wanted to and didn't need it to be in front of my eyes at a certain season.

I never paint on the spot but may make a few notes in a sketchbook as it is the overall feeling I want to express and this is best done in my studio. My eye has seen and my brain registered how the waves break against the rocks, how the clouds gather and design themselves into moving masses, how the patterns of deposits from the sea add to the textures and colors on the beach, and how the snow camouflages the regular land and seascapes making unpredictable designs. All these and more I store in my memory bringing them to use when I paint a scene so that what I paint is the essence and not a copy; in other words, a creative, living, work.

1. Take a sketchbook or paper with you on a walk or trip to the beach, woods, mountains, city, etc. Instead of drawing everything, decide on one thing you'd like to draw. Example: if you go to the coast maybe draw just the way the lobster pots look bobbing in the water and don't worry about drawing the water, the air, the boats or anything else. If you go to the mountains, maybe you will draw just the way smoke is coming out of everyone's chimneys and don't worry about drawing the houses or anything else. If it is summer maybe you can draw the flowers in a field and how they are placed, but don't worry about drawing all the grass and trees, etc.

2. After you've done these drawings look at them at the end of the day or the next day. Do they remind you of what you saw and experienced? What will you do next time to make them clearer?

Found Images

Contributed by John Muench, Artist

About this activity John Muench wrote, "...it's an interesting and fun thing to do and I sometimes use it when I'm looking for ideas."

You go about it as follows: you will need a piece of paper or board with a hard, non-absorbent surface—that is, one which will not soak up moisture. You will also need a small amount of paint thinner and a water-base paint or ink.

If you slightly moisten (*not wet*) areas of the board with thinner and then "Float in" ink or paint (quite wet) it will settle into strange patterns. *Don't* try to control it! This is known as a "resist" technique.

When the ink or paint dries you may find strange and interesting figures and designs. These are known as "found images". You may develop them further with pen and ink or color and unwanted areas can be blocked out with opaque white paint.

Try it, it can be very interesting!

Writing

Contributed by Dianne Ballon, Artist

I started keeping a journal in hope that I would advance
in my writing, that if I wrote regularly I would begin
to refine exactly what I wanted to say.
I wrote about the things I love: a cloud stretched over
a freezing pond on a clear frozen morning, the flight of
a hawk, the one or two hay wagons at the edge of a
cultivated field—all things that interest me for
their "nature" and beauty.
I found myself describing the same type of experience in
the same way: whether the cloud stretched over a pond,
a river or nestled in the valleys—it was easy to use the
same words to describe them. So I hunted for new words
which was challenging but made me feel better about
my writing.
That's how it is with things that are beautiful—
they are indescribable until you begin to describe them.

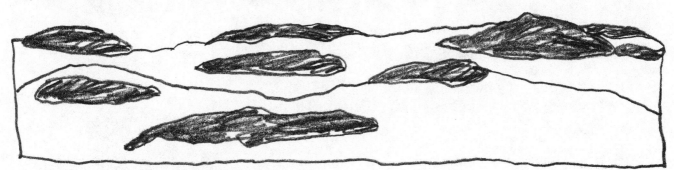

Here are the clouds engulfing the valleys.
Only the dark shapes of mountain peaks appear—
like ships in a sea of white.

Try to describe an indescribable place.

Make a Maine Logo

Contributed by Joanne Arnold, Illustrator-Designer

To make a logo for the State of Maine I think of things that remind me of Maine, pictures in my mind that without any words will mean Maine when someone else looks at them.

Now think, what is Maine to you? Maybe Maine is a seagull on a dock surrounded by the Gulf of Maine and big white puffy clouds...

or maybe it is a single white birch...

or maybe a forest of pine trees silhouetted by a full moon...or maybe Maine means moose, lobsters, blueberries and potatoes to you!

1. Make a list of things that Maine means to you. Go out and really look at the things you have listed. You might discover something you've never noticed before that can help your drawing.

Maine means:

Drawings (use extra paper if necessary)

2. Now make a Maine logo. Try to make it simple and clear using only the lines and shapes you think are important. Keep re-drawing it until you are happy with the final drawing.

It might be fun to have a whole class do these and have a "show" afterwards of everyone's logo, or even better, have everyone in the class do different states, omitting the name on the logo and have the class guess which is which.

Stories Waiting to be Written

Contributed by Ruth Sargent, Writer

Ruth Sargent believes that every spot where humans live contains exciting stories waiting to be discovered and written: stories of people who lived unusual lives and accomplished something that altered a phase of history. This sort of writing involves research which is actually detective work. She knows because she has written the book *Abbie Burgess: Lighthouse Heroine.* The story is about a fourteen-year-old girl who tended the lamps of a lighthouse off the coast of Maine. She became a legend among seamen and throughout all of New England because of her bravery during the bad storms of 1856 and 1857. Ruth Sargent has also written two other books: *The Littlest Lighthouse* and *Gail Laughlin: ERA's Advocate.*

Maine cities, towns and villages didn't "just happen". They began with the first settlers that came there to live and saw great possibilities in its location. They described the place in such a way that other people wanted to come and settle here.

1. Who were the first people in your community: farmers, miners, fishermen, ranchers? Can you find out about some of these people in the library or by asking a local history group?

Person's name _____

Where he or she lived _____

When he or she lived _____

What did the person do? _____

_____

2. Do some research and write down some interesting happenings in this person's life.

3. Create a short story of this person telling how you believe they might have been.

Getting Started in Poetry

Contributed by Walter Sargent, Poet

Start where you stand, that is, by reading or listening to some poems a friend enjoys. Poetry is a two-person game. It builds bridges between (1) the WRITING POET, who sees or thinks of something he wants to share with a (2) READING POET, eager for a new experience. Writer and reader are equally important in poetry because only at that moment when a reader says, "That is just the way I feel or see it," that a combination of the writer's sentences become a poem.

Poetry is as close to you as the pencil in your hand, or, as one poet said it, "the taste of apple on your tongue." In school days I wondered how to pick a subject for a poetry assignment. I thought these poetic lines of Carl Sandburg's were a simple example to follow:

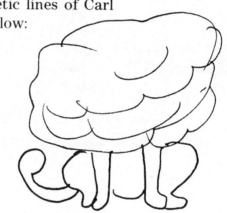

FOG
The fog comes
on little cat feet.
It sits looking
over harbor and city
on silent haunches
and then moves on. (C.S.)

But how did he pick such a subject?

It was a warm October day. In my puzzlement I sat in a sunny corner. A tickling on my hand aroused me. It was a fluffy milkweed seed. My strong desire to imitate Carl Sandburg made it easy to start thinking and writing his way:

THOUGHTS
I rested in a sunny corner.
A milkweed seed drifted near,
It spiraled from my hasty grasp;
I found that I held...nothing!
So, were my thoughts.

Another floss drifted by.
Slowly, deliberately I reached
and plucked it from the air.
I held a silken treasure!
So, were my thoughts. (W. F. S.)

Notice how in both poems two very different things (FOG and CATS; MILKWEEK SEED and A BOY EAGER FOR AN IDEA) were placed together to express a new, unexpected idea.

Poetry can be a fun craft for many. It grows easily from a love of life. Like all crafts, there are tools to sharpen your skill:

- The example of others
- dictionaries
- a thesaurus
- Simple rules of meter, rhyme, form
- ... and don't forget to revise, or the "read it aloud" test

But remember:

POETRY CONNECTS

   /   /   / /   /   /   /
I did not need an intercom to reach my reading friend,
But just a new found thought in lines that were quite simply penned.
I knew these lines did not deserve reward in coin of gold
But HIS SMILE, when he took my poem to heart, was pleasure to behold.
(WFS)

I wrote *POETRY CONNECTS* to explain one reason for writing a poem. The secret is in the fourth line. I marked the accents (feet) in line 1. Perhaps you can find and count them in the other lines. This form of poetry should have (almost always) the same number in each line so the reader will not hesitate or stumble.

Free verse doesn't "march" like *POETRY CONNECTS*, but flows in phrases in *FOG* and *THOUGHTS*. We are free to pick the kind we like—almost like choosing a picture in a frame or without.

1. Write a free verse poem that expresses something you feel or think. It will be helpful to sit or walk quietly and observe the things around you. You might find a connection between what you observe and how you feel.

Artistic License

Contributed by Sheila Gardner, Artist

A camera, perhaps, can look at the world objectively. A human being must look at the world subjectively. 'Artistic license', then, is a shorthand term for the method by which the artist presents a subjective view of the world, emphasizing those aspects which are most important to the artist.

In the case of this drawing, I have taken tracks, which in actuality were scattered over a large area, and have concentrated them. Such a concentration might well be improbable, but since it is not impossible, I feel my rearrangement is a legitimate device.

A. Abominable Snowman
B. dog
C. cat
D. raccoon
E. deer
F. rabbit
G. bird (grouse?)

1. Add additional tracks to this scene made by other animals.

2. Make your own drawing of anything—people; a view from your window, etc. Use your own "artistic license" by emphasizing or giving importance to the things in your drawing that are most important to you. You can emphasize things in many ways: by making them bigger than all the other things, or bolder, or by coloring only the emphasized things. Or, use your imagination. How can you bring more attention to one thing in your drawing than another?

Your Favorite Childhood Pet

Contributed by Jamie Wyeth, Painter

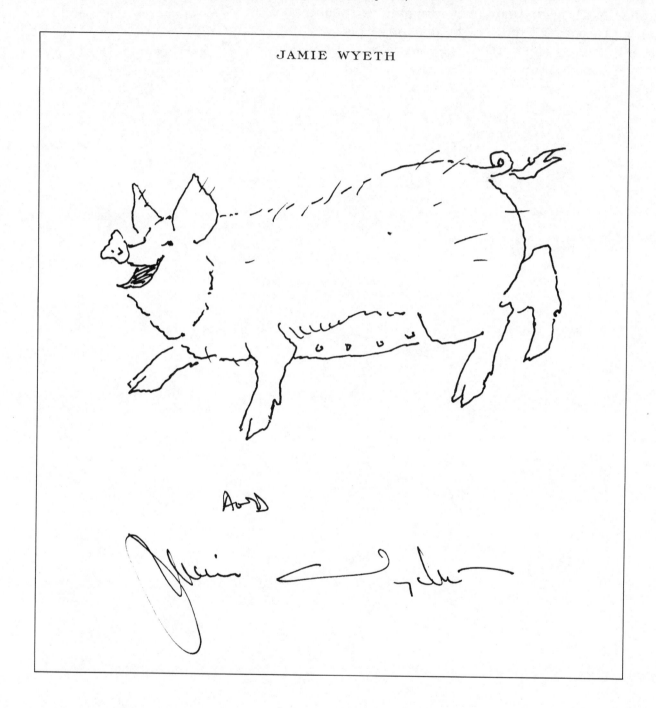

JAMIE WYETH

This playful pig was drawn by Jamie Wyeth for this book. It could be his favorite childhood pet, a large sow with a crooked nose named Den Den.

Draw a picture of your favorite animal or pet below.

In your picture try to describe the animal's personality and character. One way to do this is to exaggerate the things about your animal that really stand out. For instance: Does your cat ever appear to be smiling? Well then, draw your cat with a great big smile, or a devilish smile, or whatever. Instead of trying to draw "realistically" try and capture the animal's special character.

Make Your Own Seaside Adventure

Contributed by Mimi Carpenter

Just for fun—write and illustrate your own seaside adventure, making yourself the main "Maine" character—a mermaid or a merlad.

1. Draw yourself on this page as a mermaid or merlad. Include some other sea creatures which might be your friends.

2. Now think of an idea for a short story about you and your adventures as a mermaid or merlad on the Maine coast. Add your friends. Think of different people or things that could be enemies of these oceanside characters.

3. Draw a picture of how you imagine you and your friends in your short story.

4. Make your story into a book as you make up more adventures.

Maine Folk Songs

Contributed by Bill Bonyun, Folksinger

From the very beginning, at the time of the earliest settlers, the colonists of the District of Maine were a singing people. To begin with they brought with them from the Old Country hundreds of songs and ballads handed down to them from their parents, grandparents, great-grandparents and many generations more—deep into the past when there were no newspapers, no printing presses—when news was spread, word-of-mouth, by minstrels and bards, traveling from town to town, singing the news to the gathered townspeople. They sang in order to be heard; shouting was much too painful for the throat. Thus these old ballads were the news stories of long ago.

As soon as they were settled in their Maine homes these new Americans began making up songs describing their own colonial experiences. And to add to it, Maine, with her coastline almost three thousand miles long, became the great ship building colony—ships manned by skilled Maine sailors who created songs of their own life at sea. And Maine, with her great forests, supplied the logs with which to build these ships—logs cut, hauled and driven down the rivers by skilled Maine woodsmen who made up many songs describing their adventurous lives.

The songs of these hardy people, handed down to us—father to son, mother to daughter—are truly precious gifts from Maine, which help us understand our past in a way no history book can tell it.

The Lumberman's (Shantyboy's) Alphabet

A is for Axe, and that we all know,
And B is for Boy who can use it also.
C is for Chopping that first we begin,
And D is for Danger we often fall in.

CHO: So merry, so merry are we.
      No mortals on earth are as happy as we.
      To me I derry O derry I derry down.
      Use shantyboys well and there's nothing goes wrong.

E is for Echo that through the woods rang,
And F is for Foreman the head of our gang.
G is for Grindstone at night we do turn,
And H is for Handle that's so smoothly worn.

I is for Iron with which we mark pine,
And J is for Jolly boys all in a line.
K is for Keen edge our axes we keep,
And L is for Lice that keep us from sleep.

M is for Moss that chinks up our camp,
And N is for Needle for mending our pants.
O is for Owl a-hooting at night,
And P is for Pine that we always fall right.

Q is for Quickness we set ourselves to,
And R is for River we haul our logs to.
S is for Sled that we haul our logs on,
And T is for Team that pulls them along.

U is for Uses we put ourselves to,
And V is for Valley we haul our logs through.
W for Woods that we leave in the Spring,
And now I have sung all that I'm going to sing.

The Lumberman's (Shantyboy's) Alphabet

I have put the appropriate chords in the music score for the songs in case someone wants to accompany the songs on a piano, autoharp or guitar. But instruments weren't used for these songs long ago. The Shakers danced to their songs, the lumbermen simply never used instruments for their singing, and sailors couldn't keep this kind of instrument on their damp old wooden ships. But that doesn't mean that we can't use them.

"The Lumberman's Alphabet" I first learned from the singing of Donald Friend, a Maine lumberman who I met at Old Sturbridge Village in 1955. I have seen several printed variants since that time, the one most similar to Mr. Friend's in a book by William Doerflinger entitled "Shantymen and Shantyboys", MacMillan Company, N.Y., 1951. It is a very old song, going back at least a hundred and fifty years, very popular among Maine woodsmen.

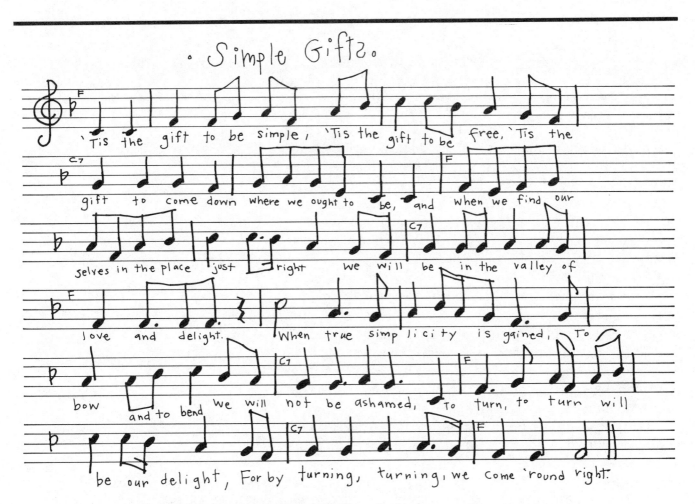

Simple Gifts

'Tis the gift to be simple, 'Tis the gift to be free, 'Tis the gift to come down where we ought to be, and when we find our selves in the place just right we will be in the valley of love and delight. When true simplicity is gained, To bow and to bend we will not be ashamed, To turn, to turn will be our delight, For by turning, turning, we come 'round right.

I learned "Simple Gifts" from Evelyn Wells, who at that time was head of the English department at Wellesley College. She had spent part of her girlhood in a Shaker colony, and she described to me her own experience watching the Shakers dance as they sang this song. Composed in Alfred or New Gloucester, Maine, 1848.

1. See if you can make an alphabet song of your own, maybe another one of the forest, naming trees, plants, animals. Or perhaps you could make one about fish in the sea, or about farming or such trades as the blacksmith, cooper, shoemaker, wheelwright.

2. Or you might try an alphabet song about your own life, your family, pets, friend's house or town. Or you can use the same tune and make up a song without the alphabet. People have always put new words to old tunes.

And since "Simple Gifts" is a New Gloucester song, made up by the Shakers in 1848, why not use that tune for your own song. After all, in far-off England someone took your New Gloucester tune to make his own song, "Lord of the Dance". Why shouldn't you?

3. For more folk songs look for books in your library.

Fame in Maine

Contributed by Bob Niss, Writer

Many women and men from Maine are famous. Robert E. Peary was the first person to reach the North Pole (other than Santa Claus, of course). Joshua Chamberlain was a Civil War general who may have won the war for the North. Margaret Chase Smith was the first Republican woman elected to the Senate and the first woman to have her name placed in nomination for the Presidency by a major party. George Gore, who had the interesting nickname "Piano Legs", was the first "hold-out" in the history of major league baseball. Harriet Beecher Stowe wrote *Uncle Tom's Cabin* in Brunswick.

Think about why and how people become famous. They do important or heroic things, but why? Do they work harder or think better than other people? Are they braver or maybe even just lucky?

Look up one of these people...or another famous Maine person...in an encyclopedia or history book and learn more about her or him.

Marsden Hartley	**Kenneth Lewis Roberts**
Henry Knox	**James Gillespie Blaine**
Dorothea Dix	**E. B. White**
Hannibal Hamlin	**Francis Edgar Stanley**
Winslow Homer	**Robert Coffin**
Edna St. Vincent Millay	**Sarah Orne Jewett**
Hiram Maxim	**Edward Arlington Robinson**
Henry Wadsworth Longfellow	**Mary Ellen Chase**
Edmund Muskie	**Nathaniel Hawthorne**

1. Which person did you pick?

2. Write some information about this person.

3. Draw a picture of this person doing what made her or him famous.

4. Many people think they would like to be famous. Famous people get lots of attention. Some of them are rich. Would you like to be famous? Draw a picture of you doing something that would make you famous.

PLAY "THE FAME GAME"

You will need a watch or clock and each player should have a pen or pencil and a piece of paper. In 10 minutes, see who can write down the most names of famous people. They can be from anywhere in the world, from just this country, or only from Maine, but you decide before the game starts. Also decide if they must be only living people or if famous people from history can be included.

Each full name (first name and last name) counts as 10 points. If you can think of only the last name, you get 5 points. First names do not count for anything by themselves. Each name should be that of a real person, not a name used in show business or a nickname: "Hawkeye Pierce" from the television show "M*A*S*H" does not count, but Alan Alda does because that is the actor's real name.

You can make the game harder by giving 5 extra points each time a player can write down something about a famous person. For instance, give 5 extra points if someone writes "Alan Alda, actor" or "Charles Lindbergh first person to fly across the Atlantic Ocean."

You can play the game by yourself, trying to get better each time or you can play against others or even pick teams to compete against each other.

Have fun!

Draw a Trip to the Beach

Contributed by Cissy Buchanan, Painter

Here is a drawing of Old Orchard Beach in 1900. How are things different today? Draw a picture of a trip to the beach you took, and include details that will suggest that it is the present. For example—What are people wearing? What are they doing? What kind of buildings and cars are around the beach? Etc.

OLD ORCHARD BEACH 1900

OLD ORCHARD BEACH 1900

cissy Buchanan

So, You want to be a Writer?

Contributed by Lew Dietz, Writer

Just about every girl and boy at one time or another has wished to become a writer. How does one go about becoming a writer? I've been asked that question time and again. The answer is simple. You write and keep on writing. There is no other way, no magic formula. There may be such a thing as a born writer, but you may be sure that for every born writer ten thousand are made by hard work and desire. It helps to have talent or at least an aptitude; but that is not enough. The creative mind like one's muscle must be exercised. You learn to play ball or jump rope by playing ball or jumping rope. You learn writing by writing.

Of all the creatures on this earth, only man possesses those symbols we call language. Learning to use these precious symbols to communicate to others our thoughts and feelings is the very essence of the writing process. And remember, though you may not succeed in making writing your career, the effort is not wasted. Whatever you do with your future, continued effort to write clearly, correctly and interestingly will enrich your lives and stand you in good stead no matter what road you choose to follow.

1. Write about what you did today, *even if* it was just another ordinary, regular day. How can you describe things around you, or describe your feelings or thoughts or the feelings and thoughts of those around you so that your story is interesting? What if you wrote about your day through the eyes of your dog or cat? What would you imagine them to think about what you do each day? What is *their* opinion of you leaving them for most of the day? Or how does your bicycle see your routine day? Or your books and pencils, etc.?

2. After writing your story, illustrate it. If you do a story from the eyes of someone or something besides yourself, keep in mind how they (or it) would see the world. Example: A small dog has to look *up* at you. How do things look different when you look up in the same way from the floor? Draw them as you see them.

Write your own story here.

Making A Calendar

Contributed by Nikki Schumann, Poster Artist

Ideas for January

·sun·mon·tues·wed·thurs·fri·sat·

Making A Calendar

Contributed by Nikki Schumann, Poster Artist

Ideas for February

·sun· mon· tues· wed · thurs· fri · sat·

Making A Calendar

Contributed by Nikki Schumann, Poster Artist

Ideas for March

·sun·mon·tues·wed·thurs·fri·sat·

Making A Calendar

Contributed by Nikki Schumann, Poster Artist

Ideas for April

·sun·mon·tues·wed·thurs·fri·sat·

Making A Calendar

Contributed by Nikki Schumann, Poster Artist

Ideas for May

·sun·mon·tues·wed·thurs·fri·sat·

Making A Calendar

Contributed by Nikki Schumann, Poster Artist

Ideas for June

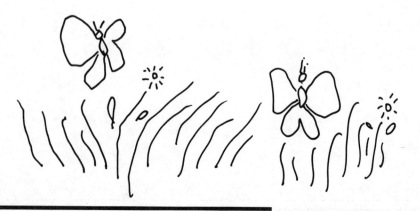

·sun·mon·tues·wed·thurs·fri·sat·

Making A Calendar

Contributed by Nikki Schumann, Poster Artist

Ideas for July

·sun·mon·tues·wed·thurs·fri·sat·

Making A Calendar

Contributed by Nikki Schumann, Poster Artist

Ideas for August

·sun·mon·tues·wed·thurs·fri·sat·

Making A Calendar

Contributed by Nikki Schumann, Poster Artist

Ideas for September

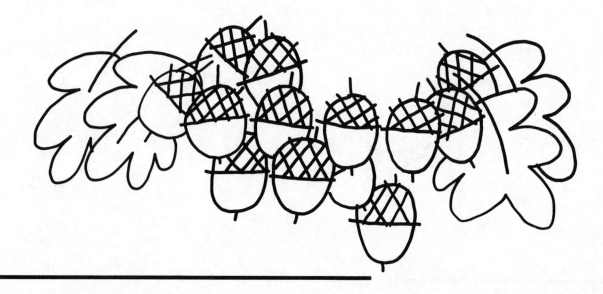

·sun·mon·tues·wed·thurs·fri·sat·

Making A Calendar

Contributed by Nikki Schumann, Poster Artist

Ideas for October

·sun·mon·tues·wed·thurs·fri·sat·

Making A Calendar

Contributed by Nikki Schumann, Poster Artist

Ideas for November

·sun·mon·tues·wed·thurs·fri·sat·

Making A Calendar

Contributed by Nikki Schumann, Poster Artist

Ideas for December

·sun·mon·tues·wed·thurs·fri·sat·

Friends of the Class
Who Encouraged This Book

A & M Rubber Supply Co., Lewiston
Agway Fertilizer, Auburn
All Points Travel, North Windham
Ames Farm Center, North Yarmouth
A Plus Floors, Gray
Barbara Hawthorne, New Gloucester
Barnhouse Tavern, North Windham
Bates Fabrics, Lewiston
Bea Libby, New Gloucester
Betty Sambor, New Gloucester
Canteen Service Co., South Portland
Casco Bank, Portland
Casco Bay Motors, Yarmouth
Central Maine Power Co., Portland
Cherryfield Foods, Cherryfield
Chrislynn Engineering, New Gloucester
Cliff's Barber Shop, New Gloucester
Coca Cola Co., Lewiston
Cole Farms Restaurant, Gray
Conifer Industries (Kentucky Fried Chicken),
     New Gloucester
Cook's Country Store, Gray
Country Sea Food, North Windham
Curry Copy Center, Lewiston
Dave's Market, Auburn
Dick's Exxon, Gray
Doghouse, Auburn
Farmstead Press, Freedom
Floyd Ray Real Estate, Auburn
Frozen Custard, New Gloucester
Future Foods, Auburn
George Elliot Advertising Inc., Portland
Gray Kiwanis Club, Gray
Gray Pharmacy, Gray
Gray Senior Citizens, Gray
Ground Round, South Portland
Hamilton & Sons Sheet Metal, Auburn
Hannaford Bros., South Portland
Hancock Lumber, Casco
Hu-Ke-Lau, South Portland
Humpty Dumpty, Scarboro
Hu Shangs, Portland
International Caterers, South Portland
Irene Levasseur, Lewiston

Jess & Nick's Variety Store, Gray
LaVerdiere's Drug Stores
Leighton's Store, New Gloucester
Leslie Peaco, New Gloucester
Levinsky's, Portland
Liberty Oil, Gray
Lost Valley, Auburn
McDonald's, North Windham
Maine Mariners
Mark Stimson Real Estate, Gray
Merrill Transport, Portland
Muddy Rudder Restaurant, Yarmouth
Naples Packing Co., Mexico
National Sea Products, Rockland
Neo-Kraft Signs, Lewiston
New England Tel. & Tel., Portland
New Gloucester P.T.O.
Oakhurst Dairy, Portland
Peoples Bank, Portland
Pine Tree Telephone Co., Gray
Porteous Mitchell & Braun, Auburn
Quoddy Moccasins, Auburn
Royal River Orchards, New Gloucester
S.D. Warren, Westbrook
Seltzer & Rydholm, Portland
Shaws Super Markets
Statler Tissues, Augusta
Stitches & Stuff, New Gloucester
Sugarloaf Ski Area, Kingfield
Sunday River Ski Area, Bethel
Thos. Moser Cabinet Makers, New Gloucester
United Society of Shakers, New Gloucester
Village Store, New Gloucester
Webb Electric, New Gloucester
Webber Oil, Portland
W.E. Cloutier Co., Lewiston
W.D. Matthews Machinery Co., Auburn
Wendy's, Auburn
Westbrook Auxiliary 197, Westbrook
Western Maine Nurseries, Fryeburg
Wild Water Adventures, Skowhegan
Windy Willow Farm, New Gloucester
Wings Variety Store, New Gloucester
World Travel, Portland

Notes

Notes